The First Year: A Marble Grant Novel

Ghost Diet & Other Marble Grant Stories

Ashes to Weddings & Other Marble Grant Stories

A Big Twisted Plot & Other Marble Grant Stories

Packet Jones

The Big Tom: A Packet Jones Short Novel

Big Eyes: A Packet Jones Short Novel

THUNDER MOUNTAIN

Thunder Mountain

Monumental Summit

Avalanche Creek

The Edwards Mansion

Lake Roosevelt

Warm Springs

Melody Ridge

Grapevine Springs

The Idanha Hotel

The Taft Ranch

Tombstone Canyon

Dry Creek Crossing

Hot Springs Meadow

Green Valley

SEEDERS UNIVERSE

Dust and Kisses: A Seeders Universe Prequel Novel

Against Time

Sector Justice

Morning Song

The High Edge

Star Mist

Star Rain

Star Fall

Starburst

Rescue Two

COLD POKER GANG

Kill Game

Cold Call

Calling Dead

Bad Beat

Dead Hand

Freezeout

Ace High

Burn Card

Heads Up

Ring Game

Bottom Pair

The Secrets of Yesterday & Other Poker Boy Stories

Dean Wesley Smith

Contents

INTRODUCTION

The title story of this collection gives a look back at the history of Las Vegas. As a fan of Vegas and it's wild and crazy history, that was a lot of fun for me to write.

And I put in some fun cookies for Poker Boy fans. At least they were fun for me.

The last story in the collection is another story about one of Lady Luck's daughters off in a world that explains a lot of the history of the gods and superheroes.

In fact, most of the stories in this collection give history about a god or a superhero or in one case, a want-to-be superhero.

Poker Boy's famous invisible office floating a thousand feet over the Las Vegas Strip plays a large part in most of these stories as well. It would be a really fun place to have lunch, that's for sure.

Sometimes, when I look out my writing office window over the Strip, I catch a glimmering of it when the sun is just right.

Hope you enjoy the stories.

DEAN WESLEY SMITH
LAS VEGAS, NEVADA

The Secrets of
Yesterday & Other
Poker Boy Stories

THE SECRETS OF YESTERDAY

CHAPTER ONE

From my office floating a thousand feet over the MGM Grand Casino and Hotel in Las Vegas, the city and surrounding area seemed painted in light brown. I could almost see the heat shimmering off the concrete and streets below as the record temperatures continued for a third day.

For a change I was alone in this office that I had designed to look like a booth in a fifties retro diner. All four walls were clear and the red vinyl booth sat in the middle of the room, two fake trees behind it to give it a feel of containment.

I had put in a wooden railing in front of the glass walls all the way around because it felt like I could fall off the edge of my office floor. Before I put those railings in I couldn't even walk near the edge. Just too creepy.

The place was invisible to anyone from below and there

were only three ways to get here. You either had to teleport, which I knew how to do, or go through the door from my girlfriend and sidekick Patty Ledgerwood's apartment. But most of the team entered through the secret door from The Diner off Freemont Street in downtown Vegas.

This office looked exactly like a booth in The Diner, actually. We used to meet there when dealing with a problem, so when I built this office, it just felt right to make it look like the old booth in The Diner.

Most everyone on my team except Stan used The Diner entrance. Patty tended to either come with me, or use the door from her apartment.

At the moment I was waiting for Patty and we were going to head to dinner, but she didn't get off work at the MGM Grand Hotel front desk for another twenty minutes.

It felt kind of odd being here alone. Normally at least three or four of the team were with me, talking about one thing or another.

And Madge, from The Diner, was always coming in and out serving us milkshakes and burgers.

At times the room had held up to fifteen people, but Madge had had to bring chairs from The Diner for that. The booth only held eight when we crowded in, and three chairs could be pulled up at the head of the table.

Right now I sat in a chair, my feet up on the wood railing around the room, facing downtown Las Vegas.

What a view. It just didn't get any better.

I felt about as relaxed as I ever could feel as a superhero

always chasing down one bad person or another. Usually I only felt this relaxed while playing poker.

Suddenly one of my faint alarms in the back of my head went off.

As a poker player, before I had become a superhero, I had learned to trust those alarms. They warned me when I was up against another player who had better cards or who might be cheating or who was getting angry.

I called the feelings my "super powers" back then. Little did I know that many of them actually were superpowers. All I had done was learn to trust them.

This time my little voice was telling me someone was watching me.

But at the same time I knew that wasn't possible. I was in an invisible office floating a thousand feet over the Las Vegas Strip. No one could see this place.

As Stan, my boss and the God of Poker, told me one day, the office was slightly out of phase with the real world. A plane trying to land at the nearby McClaren airport could fly through the office and no one would notice.

I expect that if I saw a plane coming directly at this place I would notice.

So who could be watching me now?

And why was my little voice considering that a threat?

A God of something or other might be able to see the office.

Or maybe another powerful superhero like me.

But not many others.

In fact, no one else that I could think of.

I stood and stared in the direction of downtown Vegas. The new Rush Tower of the Golden Nugget stood above most of the buildings there, but I still had to look down on it from my height.

My little voice was telling me that tower was where the problem was coming from.

And I didn't like this at all. Not one little bit.

Chapter Two

"Stan?" I shouted upward as I always did when calling my boss.

Stan appeared almost instantly beside me, also looking out toward the downtown area.

He had on his normal gray slacks, gray shirt and sweater and had his brown hair combed perfectly. He was the most nondescript man I had ever known. You could walk right past him in a hallway and never notice him, which was one thing that made him so deadly on a poker table.

I had yet to sit across from him at a poker table, and honestly had no desire to do so any time in the near future.

"You feeling it as well?" I asked as he stared at the downtown area.

"Someone's watching," he said. "And they are not blocking the fact that they are watching."

"That's why I could sense it?" I asked.

He nodded.

"Can you get a spot on the location?"

"A suite on the 25th Floor of the Golden Nugget. Corner suite. The person is staring at us?"

"Suggestions?"

"I'm going to jump us there and take us out of time," Stan said.

I nodded and a moment later we were standing in a large suite on the top floor of the Golden Nugget. The place was decorated in brown tones, with a large brown couch and chairs in an area under a large screen television.

A made king-sized bed filled another part of the huge room, with a brown comforter and white pillows. A large vanity with a marble surface faced the bed with a desk and another large flat-screened television.

Someone was in the bathroom to my right, pocket-doors slid closed.

And standing in front of the window facing in the direction of my floating office over the strip was a teenager, not more than sixteen at the most.

He was frozen, his hand holding open the drape, as was the newscaster on the television screen, since Stan had taken us out of time.

Actually, I knew how to do that as well. It was more that he had slipped us between two instants of time, but it had the affect of seeming to stop time for anyone taken out of time.

The kid was dressed like most normal teenagers with jeans

and a blue tee-shirt not tucked in. His hair was cut short and he looked like he played sports because his shoulders were broad and he didn't have an ounce of fat on him.

"He's powerful," Stan said, nodding at the kid. "I can feel it."

Actually, I could as well. "Is this unusual for someone his age?"

"Very," Stan said, his voice serious.

"Can he sense us here?" I asked.

"He might be able to."

"I can hear you as well," the kid said, turning to look at us.

His face was angular and his eyes a deep black. And as he turned just about every alarm I had as a superhero went off in my head.

More than anything I just wanted to jump and run. But Stan stayed put beside me and so I did the same, my best poker face firmly in place.

"You were looking for us?" Stan asked, his voice as neutral as it always seemed.

"I was," the kid said, nodding and moving away from the window. He moved past us and sat on the couch. "Actually, I was looking for more people of my kind. Guess I found a few, huh? That your place out there floating over the Strip?"

I nodded and said nothing more. At this point, I was glad, more than glad, to let Stan handle this.

"So who are you?" Stan asked.

"Jason King," the kid said. "My mom, Bonnie, is in the

bathroom. She doesn't have any of these powers I have, or at least doesn't seem to."

"Oh, I do, dear," a voice said as the pocket doors to the bathroom slid back. "I just never let you know about them."

I glanced around.

Stan still held us in a time bubble. The newscaster on the television was still stuck in mid sentence and outside the window I could see a jetliner headed for McClarin just hanging there in mid-air. And there were no sounds coming from the city around us at all.

Yet two people had broken into the time bubble Stan had set as if it were nothing unusual. I couldn't do that and I was supposedly one of the most powerful superheroes out there.

Or maybe no one had taught me how to do that yet.

"Hi, Stan," the woman said as she came around the corner in the suite from the bathroom area.

She was attractive and thin and looked to be about the same age as all the Gods and superheroes, mid-thirties. It seems we all pretty much stopped aging at that point for some reason or another.

She had long brown hair pulled back off her face and dark brown eyes. She wore a red summer dress and was barefoot. And she was smiling, but I wasn't sure the smile was reaching her eyes or not.

"Bonnie?" Stan asked, actually sounding shocked.

I glanced at my boss. He was the God of Poker. Even when something shocked him, he never showed it. He was the master of poker faces. But right now he was showing surprise just as any normal human would.

This time the smile actually did reach her eyes. And there was more there. A love, a fondness.

"It's great to see you again," she said, moving over and taking his hands and then reaching up and kissing him on the cheek.

"But I thought... I thought..." Stan couldn't seem to finish his sentence.

"That we were dead," she asked, still smiling. "We were."

"And it wasn't a lot of fun, either," Jason said, dropping onto the couch and putting his feet up on the coffee table.

Stan stared first at Bonnie, then looked at Jason. Then back at Bonnie with a questioning look.

I was reading Stan's face. In the years I had worked for him, that had never happened. Not once.

"Is he...?" Stan asked.

Bonnie nodded. "Jason," she said, turning to her son slouched on the couch. "I would like you to meet your biological father, Stan, the God of Poker."

"So," Jason said, nodding, but not acting surprised or shocked. "He's the guy who killed us."

Chapter Three

The silence in the room couldn't have been cut with a chainsaw.

I moved silently over and dropped onto a chair near the vanity, doing my best to just pretend I wasn't here. I had no idea what was happening, what had happened between Bonnie and Stan, and not a clue why Jason scared me to death.

This all seemed way, way out of my league at the moment. I really, really, really needed someone to spend some time filling me in on the history of all this, including the history of the people I worked with. I had only been a superhero now for a short ten years. I was an open book, but it sure seemed that everyone around me had a lot of history and secrets.

"I didn't..." Stan said, shaking his head, clearly upset and clearly surprised at meeting his son.

"Oh, we know you didn't," Bonnie said, smiling at Stan. "Don't we, Jason?"

"Yeah, whatever," he said, shrugging like any teenager.

Bonnie smiled again, but this time the smile once again didn't reach her eyes.

Every alarm in my body went off again.

I focused all my powers and without saying a word out loud, I shouted the thought, *Laverne!*

Watching. Her voice came back strong in my head. *And no need to shout.*

Laverne was Lady Luck herself, one of the most powerful Gods there was. I felt a lot better with her watching this. Whatever this was.

Stan shook his head and then regained his calm poker face. "If you didn't die, then where have you been for the last sixteen years?"

"Oh, we did die," Bonnie said.

"Buried," Jason said.

I almost shuddered at the very idea, but managed to stay still, tucked off on the side in my chair.

"Buried?" Stan asked. "How can that be? I saw the cabin burn to the ground with you in it. I couldn't get to you and couldn't stop the flames."

"Did you find a body?" Bonnie asked.

Stan shook his head. "The magic in those flames took everything down to fine ashes. I killed Crystal for what she did to you."

Holy smokes. Stan killed someone?

Bonnie nodded, clearly sad. "I know you did. And I know what that cost you."

Don't ask, Laverne's voice said softly in my head before I could even form a thought about asking Stan what had happened later. *Don't ever ask him. Ever.*

Understood.

"I had crawled under the floorboards of the cabin," Bonnie said, her voice soft. "I dug down into the mud and soft dirt, but I still died. And our unborn child, Jason, died with me."

"But how?" Stan asked. Then clearly, as I watched his face, he seemed to understand something. "Osiris?"

Bonnie nodded.

Laverne put in my mind an image of a tall, thin, green-skinned man wearing a white long beard and carrying a black stick. He wore robes that seemed to shimmer in the image. *One of the great old ones. The major God of Death and of Life.*

I didn't know there were great old ones.

Laverne thankfully said nothing to that stray thought by me.

Bonnie went on. "Osiris took my remains while the flames were still hot and put me in an ancient wooden coffin in an old cemetery in Boise, Idaho. The previous resident had gone mostly to dust. In there, in that darkness, Osiris slowly let life come back into my body."

"I was born in that coffin," Jason said, clearly disgusted. "We were in that old coffin until I was five living on worms and grubs and dripping water from above."

Now I actually did shudder. There were many things about the Gods and superheroes I had come to dislike, but whatever had happened to these two topped anything I had learned so far.

Stan's face looked white and he turned away. I had no idea how he was even holding it together. His son had been born six feet underground in a coffin. And had to stay there for five years.

"It took that long before we regenerated completely," Bonnie said softly. "But we are now alive. Osiris accepted us into his world and we live in comfort there. Osiris is training Jason."

I wanted to ask what he was training him for, but then Laverne thought *To replace him as the God of Death.*

Oh.

Stan looked at his son and then bowed slightly to him. "I did try to save you. I had no idea you survived. I owe Osiris a great debt."

Jason just sat on the couch under the window and shrugged like any bored teenage kid would do.

A moment later a very tall, very green man with a long white beard appeared beside Bonnie. He wore a silk robe that shimmered and radiated power like I had never felt before.

Suddenly the suite smelled of a beach fire and rose petals.

Laverne appeared beside him and bowed to him.

Stan bowed to him and I scrambled to my feet and did the same, stunned that Laverne would bow to anyone. Wow did I have a lot to learn about the Gods and this world I played a very small part in.

I so wanted to just jump away from this, but instead I backed up as much as I could and tried to make myself as unnoticed as possible.

Jason just sat on the couch looking bored.

Osiris faced Stan. "I am sorry I could not tell you about your wife and son. I did not know if I could save them or if they would come through the process sane."

"I am very glad you did save them," Stan said.

"We cannot return to you," Bonnie said to Stan, a sadness now in her brown eyes.

Stan nodded. "I understand."

Osiris reached over and took Bonnie's hand and it was clear they were now a couple of some sort.

Stan nodded and smiled and after a moment Bonnie also smiled.

Then something happened that I am sure would give me nightmares for years. Osiris, the God of Death and one of the ancient ones that even Laverne bowed to, turned and faced me directly.

His eyes were a swirling pool of silver and black and he seemed to have a sly grin hidden in that white beard.

"Poker Boy," he said and I swore his voice seemed to echo into all parts of my head. "I have watched you and your team save this world and the gods in it many times. I now ask for your help."

I nodded and somehow said with a slight bow, "Anything you desire, sir."

"In a few years Jason will require training in the arts of discipline and control of his emotions if he is to someday rule in my place."

On the couch Jason just snorted. I did not look away from Osiris.

"When the time comes, I would like you to teach him those arts through the game you call poker. You are the best poker player in the world. Jason will require the best."

I don't think I was breathing, but I did manage to say, "I would be honored, sir."

"Very good," Osiris said, smiling and showing me a mouthful of rotted and yellowed teeth.

He turned to Laverne. "It is always an honor."

"The honor is mine, Great One," Laverne said, bowing slightly.

Osiris then turned to Stan. "I am deeply sorry for your loss."

Stan nodded and then glanced at Bonnie with a smile. "It seems that from the ashes has come some good."

Bonnie smiled back and the smile reached her eyes. And the relief that Stan understood.

Stan was letting her go.

Osiris nodded and bowed slightly to Stan. "You are as great a young god as Bonnie led me to believe."

Then Osiris, Bonnie, and Jason were gone.

My legs gave out and I dropped down onto the chair.

Laverne stepped over to Stan and put her hand on his shoulder like a parent comforting a small child.

Then without a word they were both gone and the sounds of the city outside the suite came crashing back in as they let go of the time bubble we had all been inside.

I was now alone in a plush hotel suite trying to catch my breath. I took two deep, shuddering breaths, working to slow my heart that seemed to want to pound right out of the front of my chest.

I worked to just clear my mind and relax as I had learned to do at a poker table in times of stress.

In a moment I felt better.

I stood, went to the window, and looked out the window at my office floating there in the sky over the MGM Grand. There were still almost thirty minutes before Patty got off work. She'd never believe what had just happened. Or maybe she would.

And then I realized that I had just agreed to give the adopted son of the God of Death poker lessons.

Once again I had to sit down and try to catch my breath.

And that wasn't easy to do.

A Night With A Forgotten God

CHAPTER ONE

You would think that with all my varied superpowers, I would have one that would warn me when a really good night was about to turn into something else. Just a tingling, maybe a little buzz behind one ear, something.

But nope.

This Saturday night started off as normal as a Saturday night gets for a superhero working for the gods of gambling.

I was playing in a great no-limit game in the poker room at Spirit Winds casino. Since I was Poker Boy, and playing poker was what I also did for a living between rescuing people and saving the world, finding a good game with decent players on a Saturday night was about as good as it came.

The noise from the nearby casino was a study background

sound of people excited at the craps table and bells and alarms of slot machines.

A faint smoke smell drifted in from the casino floor where smoking was still allowed. At times I figured it was almost demanded that a person had to smoke to play a slot machine. Smoking in poker rooms had been banned a decade ago, and for that I will be forever grateful.

I had just had a snack at the free buffet that they set up in the poker room. The entire five-foot buffet was basically some crackers and cheeses and curled up vegetables of one sort or another. I stuck with the crackers and some cheese and a bottle of water. I figured that would get me to a late dinner.

The Spirit Winds poker room had fourteen tables and right now there were seven games going, with another table about to start up. The game I was in was the major game in the room, and we were tucked to one side of the big room so that people could stand and watch from the edges of the room.

Right now we had about ten people watching the play.

I loved this casino and considered it my home casino even though I spent most of my time in Las Vegas and had an invisible office floating a thousand feet over the MGM Grand Hotel and Casino. This little casino tucked off in the Oregon mountains felt like home.

I had played here before I met Stan, the God of Poker and my boss, and before I found out I was a superhero. So my roots were here.

And no one in this casino really knew anything about my

alter identity as Poker Boy. They just all called me "Hat" because of the black fedora-like hat I always wore and the black leather coat. No one in Oregon knew that hat and coat was my superhero uniform that helped strengthen my superpowers.

I loved the area of the Oregon Coast Mountains so much, I was building a huge home about a mile away from here on some land I owned. Actually, Patty Ledgerwood, aka Front Desk Girl, and I were building the home, paying a guy I had helped rescue a year or so ago.

We weren't married, but we had been an item now for years and I had a hunch the marriage thing would come at some point. We had talked about it, but since we were both superheroes, we figured taking our time wouldn't hurt. Especially since we were both basically immortal now. I still looked like I was thirty, as did all gods and superheroes. I was going on fifty in real years.

Patty wouldn't tell me her real age, but I had a hunch from some of the things she had said, she was well past one hundred years old. Thankfully, she just looked thirty as well.

The home we were building was tucked back in the trees on forty acres. When done, it would have a huge indoor pool and game room. It was being built partially out of local logs. It was costing me over two million to build and wouldn't be done for almost another year, but Patty and I loved to visit it every week or so and see the progress and just sit and stare out over the valley. The view from the new house could take your breath away at sunset and at sunrise.

Patty had been surprised I had so much money that I could afford a two-million-dollar home, and honestly I was surprised as well. I had just never really counted it up. Since I learned how to teleport, I no longer had to fly anywhere, so about all I spent my winnings on was food.

And other investments, which, it seemed, often turned out to pretty good investments.

Patty helped me figure it all out once before we started construction and the total had shocked both of us. Two million for the home wasn't going to dent how much money I had.

I had bought into the no-limit game for two hundred and in over two hours I had built that up to over a thousand. And had fun doing it, and it seemed the players around me were enjoying the game as well, which made it even better, even though they were losing.

It was still just a little before eleven in the evening. Patty worked the front desk at the MGM Grand Hotel in Vegas and I didn't have to meet her until two in the morning. So I had three more hours of play left before I had to cash out, teleport to Vegas, and go out for a late dinner with the woman of my dreams.

The noise from the nearby casino floor for a moment seemed to suddenly fade, then came back again strong.

I glanced around, but no else had noticed and I could see or feel no reason for anything like that to happen.

And none of my warning senses were going off at all.

Weird, just weird.

Then, out of the corner of my eye I caught a glimpse of a guy standing to one side of the room, just watching the game.

But he wasn't really there. More like a ghost.

I could see the wall right through him without a problem.

My wonderful Saturday night had just taken a turn onto a new road. Which road would depend on what the ghost wanted.

Chapter Two

Now, I had come to believe in a lot of things since becoming a superhero, such as aliens, old races of Titans, and powerful gods of math. But I still hadn't heard a word that ghosts were real, and I kind of still doubted they were.

With one eye on the ghost, I took myself out of time.

Around me the noise of the casino shut off, leaving the entire place instantly silent. And everyone froze in the instant.

People's faces do not belong frozen in an instant. It twists them all up into something not natural or attractive.

Jumping into an instant of time felt like I was actually stopping time, but all I was doing was moving into an instant.

Time was still going on just fine and I hadn't stopped anything. I just existed outside of the flow of time.

I stood and headed toward the ghost.

He was frozen as well, his attention focused on the table I had been playing at. He wore an old-fashioned dark cloth shirt, dark cloth pants, and a wide rope belt. Over that he had what looked like a 1800s dress jacket. He had short dark hair and no beard at all.

He stood not more than five foot tall and he looked around thirty or so.

I studied him for a moment, not having a clue what to do next.

I could see right through him, of that there was no doubt. And from the looks of a woman's face standing about five feet away, she had noticed him as well just as I froze time.

So it wasn't just my powers that saw him.

I had no idea what to do, so when that happened, I did the most logical thing.

"Stan!" I shouted at the ceiling.

I have no idea why I always shouted his name and why it was at the ceiling. Just an old habit from my first days as a superhero when I was calling for him all the time it seemed.

He appeared between me and the ghost looking like the God of Poker always looked. He had on tan slacks, a tan shirt, a slightly darker sweater without an identifying mark on any of it. His hair was cut perfectly and his face always neutral. He stood exactly five-ten, not too short and not too tall. And he seldom smiled, although over the years I had seen him shocked a few times and smile a few other times.

In other words, he was the kind of guy who could walk by

you in a hallway and most people would never remember anyone walked past them.

"Winning?" he asked.

"Of course," I said.

"So what's the problem?"

I pointed to the short ghost standing behind him.

Stan turned and then just shook his head.

"What is it?" I asked.

"Not what, who. That's Ben."

"So he's not a ghost?"

Stan shook his head and I felt relieved.

"Nope, he's a god."

Chapter Three

Of all the things Stan could told me about the nearly invisible guy wearing rumpled old-style clothing, the fact that he was a God stunned me.

And as a God, he had let me get out of time and approach him. All the Gods I had met, and that was no small number, were able to sense when someone slipped out of time around them.

"So what's he the god of?" I asked.

"Lamplighters," Stan said, his voice sad.

"Lamplighters? What's that?"

"And thus the reason for his condition," Stan said. "His entire area is being forgotten. Lamplighters used to be a huge number of men, and a few women, who went around city or town streets all over the world and lit the lamps. They reached the height of their profession in the gas-lamp era."

"There was a god for that?" I asked.

Stan gave me a dirty look. "I'm the God of Poker. There's a God for everything."

I looked at Ben the God ghost and finally caught a clue. When a god's area went away, eventually the god did as well.

"How come he couldn't shift to another area?" I asked.

"Some are able to," Stan said. "Some would rather just fade away as their area of expertise does with time."

"So what's he doing here?" I asked.

Stan shrugged. "Let's ask him."

A moment later Ben realized he had been taken out of time and that Stan and I stood there staring at him.

"Stan," Ben said, his voice not much more than a distant whisper even though he seemed to be talking normally. If we hadn't been out of time and the casino completely silent, I never would have been able to hear him.

"Ben, great seeing you again," Stan said. "Haven't found a new area that interests you yet, I am gathering?"

Ben held up his nearly see-through arms and laughed. "Yeah, pretty obvious. You know there are less than one hundred professional lamplighters left in the world?"

I almost said I was surprised there were that many, but I managed to keep my mouth shut and let Stan do the talking to someone he clearly knew out of the past.

"So what are you doing here?" Stan asked.

Ben sort of half-pointed at me. "Since I have a lot of time on my hands, I've been following Poker Boy and his team and all the good work all of you are doing. And how many times the team has saved all of us."

I nodded my thanks and again kept my mouth shut.

Stan did the same thing, so Ben went on in his whisper-sounding voice.

"So I wanted to come and see if I could get a chance to ask Poker Boy what area of expertise his team was missing and I would move in that direction with the hope that in a few hundred years or so I might have enough of my powers back to be able to help out in a crisis or two."

Areas we lacked?

I honestly hadn't given that any thought. Not one.

The team consisted of Patty, aka Front Desk Girl who had the ability to calm anyone into a smile, including me in the most stressful of times.

Screamer was an original member. He could link people's minds together and read thoughts.

We had Smoke, part wolf, part human, who could walk through walls and sense and smell things from great distances.

Madge, a superhero in the area of food service, added in her keen eye and ability to cut right to the point of something. Plus she made the best milkshakes ever made on the planet.

And then there was Stan, my boss, a God who seemed to know almost everyone, kept us all balanced, and knew were to go for help when we needed it.

We had a few others who had helped on certain missions, but that was the core. What were we missing?

A very good question.

And clearly a question that just might save Ben's life. But, one thing I didn't know about Ben. Did the powers-that-be want him saved? I had met my share of gods and not all of them were liked.

Maybe Ben's demise was something no one wanted to stop.

"That's very flattering," I said to Ben. "And let me think for a minute. And I'm going to need to talk with Stan, if you don't mind, since he's my boss in all this."

Ben smiled and meekly waved. "Oh, sure, no problem. Thanks for even considering my crazy question."

With that Stan put Ben back frozen, and we turned and walked away, waving between the people stuck in real time in varied poses.

The silence was intense and I wanted to make sure Ben couldn't hear my next question to Stan.

Finally Stan stopped near the tiny buffet of crackers and cheese and browning lettuce, frowned at it in clear disgust, and then turned to me.

"What's he like and can he hear us?" I asked.

"He barely has enough power to maintain his essence in the world," Stan said. "He can't hear us. And he's a very, very nice man, from everything I heard and know about him."

"So people would welcome him being saved?"

Stan nodded. "I don't think he has an enemy anywhere, and that's saying something with Gods."

I agreed with that. I had seen more bickering and feuding among the gods than I would have seen watching kids play on a playground during recess. With great power and years of age comes great pettiness, it seemed.

"Why didn't he just move around into other areas of city government?" I asked Stan, glancing back at the ghost that was Ben.

"He doesn't interact well with people," Stan said. "He's very shy and not strong enough for management, not physically able to handle something like garbage, and besides, there just aren't a lot of slots sometimes for a god to move to."

"So he just stayed where he was and the world went past," I said.

"Exactly," Stan said.

"I wonder what he's been doing with his time for the last hundred years?"

Stan just shrugged.

My little voice, which was part of my superpowers, kind of dinged me. The answer to Ben's problem had something to do with what he had been doing since electricity started lighting city streets.

"Let's go ask him," I said.

Stan looked puzzled, but just shrugged why not.

I turned back and weaved my way in and around the frozen people.

As we got close, Stan brought Ben out of time and into the silence of our little bubble.

Before Ben could say anything, I asked him point blank. "What have you been doing to fill your time over the last one hundred years?"

He looked down at the floor, clearly embarrassed. Then he said even softer than normal, "I read."

"Read?" I asked. "Read what?"

"Everything," he said, clearly a glow filling him slightly. "I love books, all sorts of books. I love bookstores, libraries, everything about any form of books. I even love the new electronic books."

He reached into a pocket of his loose old jacket and pulled out an electronic reader.

I glanced at Stan who seemed as shocked as I felt, but it was hard to get a read on the emotions of the God of Poker.

"How much do you remember about what you read?" I asked.

"Everything," he said. "My memory is photographic, even slipping away like this. I know which book I read what in and when and who the author was and everything. I own a large castle outside of London and it's completely full of books. I guess you would say I'm a hoarder."

I flat didn't want to think about an entire castle full of ancient books. I could easily see his passion was everything books and reading. Everything.

"When did you start this reading?"

"Gutenberg invented the press and it wasn't long after that. But I also have collected and read a lot of old scrolls and have spent many a wonderful day in the Library of Alexandria."

"That still exists?" I asked, stunned.

Beside me Stan said, "Oh, sure."

Ben nodded.

Damn I had a lot to learn about history and the gods and everything else. I really hated always being the young and stupid one in a conversation among old gods and superheroes.

Then it dawned on me what I had just thought.

Knowledge. If my team had the knowledge of history stored in Ben's head, we would be a ton stronger.

A million times stronger, actually.

I turned to Stan. "Is there a god of books, a god of libraries, a god of bookstores?"

"Yes, yes, and yes," Stan said.

"Can a god go back to being a superhero if there are no spots open?"

"Sure," Stan said, nodding and thinking.

"Good," I said. "We need to find a spot somewhere in the book world for Ben, because we need him now on the team."

Ben looked stunned and Stan just smiled.

I looked at Ben feeling how lucky we all were that all the knowledge that Ben had gathered had not just faded away with him.

"I'll be right back," Stan said.

He vanished and I smiled at Ben, who was looking stunned and very shy. I could see why he hadn't been able to stay in the city government world of Gods.

"I don't understand," he said, looking up at me.

"Do you trust me?" I asked.

He nodded.

"Do you love books and reading?"

"More than anything in the world."

"And you can remember everything you've read?"

"Everything."

I nodded. "Then the team needs you now, not a hundred years from now. So we just got to get you out of this fading-away state."

Ben was about to say something when Stan reappeared with a striking woman in a white blouse, long black skirt, and black glasses. Her shiny black hair was pulled back and tied in a bun to the back of her head. She was short, maybe five-two at the most, but she radiated power.

A lot of power, actually.

She saw Ben and instantly put a hand over her mouth in shock. "Oh, my, Ben, what's happened? You didn't move from the lamplighter position, did you?"

He just shook his head and looked down at the ground, ashamed.

"Baalat, I'd like you to meet Poker Boy," Stan said. "Poker Boy, this is Baalat, the god of all reading and books."

She turned to me and smiled. I managed to bow slightly and she extended her hand and I shook it. Her skin felt smooth and firm and her grip firm as well.

"I have heard so much about your team," she said. "We all owe you so much."

"Thank you," I said. Then somehow I managed to focus my attention away from one of the most powerful and stunning gods I had yet to meet and back to the problem at hand.

"Ben has a photographic memory for everything he has ever read since books were invented."

"You do?" Baalat asked Ben directly, looking at the ghost of a man.

Ben nodded and said nothing, still staring at the ground at his feet.

So I kept going, pitching his case. "And Ben has been reading scrolls as well from before books. And he loves electronic books. He tells me he loves all books, no matter what type or shape. He loves reading. Period."

"Is this true?" Baalat asked, looking away from me and back at Ben.

Ben this time looked up and nodded, staring into her eyes. "Completely. It's all I ever do is read. I haven't had much work to do for a very long time."

I went on. "The knowledge he holds of history and facts and lost arts in that photographic mind would be invaluable to my team and some of the major problems we face. But he needs to have a position somewhere that will allow him to regain strength. Stan and I are hoping you might have that spot available, and let him have the time to work with my team as well."

Baalat smiled at me and I darned near melted. "Poker Boy, you are as amazing as everyone says."

Then thankfully, before my knees gave out under the high-wattage smile, she turned to Ben.

"Would you like to work for me as one of the Gods of Reading and Books?"

I thought Ben was going to turn into a ghost child right in front of us, his smile was so big. "I would so much enjoy that?"

"So we need to get you transferred, but I don't think your old boss will much care, do you?"

"He's been pushing me for fifty years to find something," Ben said.

"Good," Baalat said.

Then she turned to me. "As soon as I get Ben squared away and trained in some of his new duties, I'll have him contact you."

"Thank you," I said. "But please not too long. If something big comes up, we're going to need him."

Baalat smiled. "When you need him, he will be there."

She nodded to Stan and then she and Ben vanished.

"Looks like we have a new team member," I said, smiling at Stan.

He just shook his head and patted me on the shoulder, smiling. "Now I understand why you also save stray dogs."

And with that he was gone.

I headed back over to the table, sat back down and released myself back into the flow of time.

The sounds of the casino smashed in around me.

And the wonderful Saturday night went on.

Then, to one side of the table, I caught something out of the corner of my eye.

It was ghost Ben standing there, smiling at me.

And then I saw his lips move as he clearly said, "Thank you."

And then he vanished.

And the very next hand the dealer dealt me pocket aces, so I knew Lady Luck was smiling as well.

A Storm From The Relic

A Storm from the Relic

Good poker players never really believe in luck. Good players know that luck levels out over time and that skill always wins in the long run.

But as Poker Boy, I knew luck very much existed, and I had met her many times over the years. I even saved her life once. Lady Luck, known as Laverne, was a very real and a very powerful God.

But most players, especially newer players, had never had the chance to meet Lady Luck, so they often used something lucky to try to get her attention in some way or another.

That was silly, of course. Laverne had far, far more pressing matters to deal with than rewarding some idiot for bad play because he had a polished rock on his bad cards.

But players of all types used talismans of one sort or another to put on their cards when in a hand.

There was a practical reason for it, of course. It was called "protecting your cards" in case a careless dealer tried to take them before the hand was over, or some careless person tossed their cards and hit yours. If your cards were protected with a chip or something on top of them, they were fine.

Over the years of sitting at poker tables, I had seen players use polished rocks, polished bones, chess pieces, Risk pieces, lucky tokens, and so much more.

It was almost two in the morning on a late Saturday night. Outside it was a beautiful fall evening in the Oregon Mountains. The sounds of bells ringing and excited people at the craps table drifted in from the main part of the casino along with the faint smell of smoke. It was legal to smoke on the casino floor, but not in the poker room, a rule which I was very thankful was in place.

I had only thirty minutes to keep playing in my favorite small poker room at Spirit Winds Casino before I had to teleport to Las Vegas to meet my girlfriend, Patty, aka Front Desk Girl. I had managed to get a couple thousand up for the evening. Considering how small the room was, and how few tourists were in the casino at this time of the year, I felt as if the night had been a success.

Then a man wearing a large winter coat and black stocking cap came toward the table carrying a rack of red chips worth five hundred dollars, the maximum buy-in to the table.

Normally seeing someone like that coming would get me

excited and force me to stay a few more hands to see if I could nab some of those chips.

But suddenly every danger alarm I had went off at once, almost rocking me back in my chair. I had never gone from completely calm and with no alerts to completely on alert in such short notice before.

The guy put the rack of chips on the table and took off his coat. He wore regular jeans and a plaid shirt under the big winter coat. He seemed trim and in shape.

He nodded to one of the other men at the table, took off his stocking cap and stuffed it in his coat, then hung his coat on a nearby coat tree against one wall.

I couldn't figure out what about the guy was causing the danger signals. He just seemed like a regular guy, clearly from outside the area. I had never seen him in this casino before. And considering he was about to sit down in a no-limit game with five hundred dollars, the guy clearly wasn't that worried about money.

There was nothing at all about him that seemed dangerous in the slightest.

The guy turned from his coat, then seemed to remember something and dug something small out of one of the coat pockets.

And when that item came into the light, I almost had to put my hands over my ears to try to cut down the screaming alarms of all my warning superpowers going off at once.

Everything inside me just shouted "Run!"

That was not a feeling I was used to having.

I pushed back from the table. "Got to go pick up my girl-friend," I said to the dealer.

The dealer, a nice guy named Carl, motioned for James, the room's brush to come over and rack up my chips.

I stood and stepped a few feet away from the table to try to catch my breath and think.

The guy set a golden-looking piece of metal on the table and sat down and started to stack his chips.

Whatever that thing was on the table, it was frighteningly dangerous.

The guy wasn't dangerous.

The talisman was.

How the heck was that even possible?

I froze time around myself, but it did nothing to calm my alarms. Basically what I did was just step between two moments in time, but it felt like I had frozen time since all the noise from the casino stopped and everyone looked frozen in mid-step. Besides teleportation, stepping between instants of time was my favorite superpower.

I wanted to get a better look at that talisman, but as I stepped toward it, every warning alarm I had as a superhero went off even louder than before.

And that was a lot of alarms.

I felt as if a thousand little voices were all shouting at me at once. All inside my head.

All of them shouting for me to turn and just run.

Nothing like that had ever happened before.

I staggered back like a drunk coming out of a bar at

closing time. I almost bumped into James frozen on his way toward the table with empty racks to get my chips.

"Stan!" I shouted toward the ceiling, even though I didn't need to shout upward to get his boss, the God of Poker to come running.

Stan appeared beside me and before I could get a word out he staggered slightly and spun around, staring at the table.

"What is that thing?" I asked.

Stan shook his head and pulled me a dozen more steps back away from the table.

With each step away from the talisman, the warnings faded slightly. It was no wonder the guy could get so close to the table with that thing in his pocket before I felt it. Whatever it was, it had a limited range.

"So you don't honestly know what that thing is?" I asked Stan.

Stan just shook his head. "Never felt anything like that before. But it feels very, very old."

I realized Stan was right, it did feel old. And powerful. And evil, all rolled into one tiny little shiny piece of metal.

"Can you get Ben?" I asked. "He might know what it is."

Stan nodded and vanished.

I stepped even farther away from the frozen table. Ben was an old god who loved to read. He looked like an old man you would see shuffling down the street in baggy pants and an old ill-fitting jacket. His hair was gray and very thin. He had been the god of lamplighters for centuries until that profession faded and he faded with it. I had managed to get him in with the gods of books, since he loved to read and remembered everything he had ever read since the beginning of printing and even before.

He was a gentle man and very nice and very shy. He was the newest member of my team, but so far we hadn't had a mission that we needed him on yet.

And at some point I was going to get him to show me the Library of Alexandria.

Stan and Ben appeared beside me. Ben smiled at me and I could tell he was recovering quickly from his ghost state. He looked almost solid now and much healthier, although still very thin.

He started to say something to me and then froze.

He turned in the direction of the table, staring.

"Do you know what would cause that?" I asked. "It's coming from that gold talisman on the table."

"The Relic," Ben said, his voice so soft that if I didn't have time frozen and all the noise from the casino gone, I never would have heard him.

"Oh, shit," Stan said and vanished again, leaving me standing there with Ben.

"What is the Relic?" I asked.

Ben indicated we should move even farther away from the table and I was glad to do so. We moved back so that we were almost out of the poker room and onto the casino main floor.

My danger alarms were still going off strong, but more distance from that thing eased them even more. Clearly Ben and Stan had the same kind of thing.

"The Relic was a spaceship," Ben said. "The legends have it that the ship crashed here in the early days of humans on this planet. It was filled with the vilest of evil aliens. The Titans, the Giants, and the early days of the Gods all banded together to fight the creatures of extreme power who came off that ship."

I looked at him and all I could say was, "Oh."

Ben said nothing more and I went back to staring at the table, wondering just where Stan had gone to.

Finally, my mind cleared enough so that I had another couple of questions for Ben. "How did that guy get a piece of the ship? And why is it still dangerous?"

"In the final great battle, the evil aliens were pushed back into their ship," Ben said. "With that kind of pressure, the ship exploded, scattering the ship and the aliens into millions of pieces. Every piece of the ship contained an essence of an alien. The evil creatures still inhabit the remaining pieces."

"And that's why it feels dangerous?" I asked.

"No, it doesn't just feel dangerous, it is dangerous," Ben said, his voice firm and clear. "The man who has it clearly has no magical powers, but he is being controlled by the entity in the metal. If a magical person touches that piece, the evil will escape from it and inhabit that person."

"That's happened in the past?"

Ben nodded. "Hitler."

"I thought he was a troll," I said, completely shocked.

"He was," Ben said. "Inhabited by the evil from that ancient battle."

Now I finally understood something. "That's why Hitler was always searching for more magic and religious items?"

Ben nodded. "He was looking for more of his kind to bring them back. He found a few of them before he was stopped and they were all killed."

I just stood there staring at the frozen poker table. It was common for a player to show other players their "lucky" talisman, especially if it had a cool look to it. So a poker table was a perfect place for the alien in that piece of metal to find someone even slightly magical.

"I wonder how he found it," I said out loud.

"That's the most important thing we need to learn," Ben said. "We must get that man away from that piece of the Relic to find out."

Stan and Lady Luck appeared.

She was wearing her standard business suit and had her hair pulled back tight. She turned to the table. "Oh, my," was all she said.

I had never seen Lady Luck look worried before, but right now she was clearly upset and very worried.

I looked at the table and at James frozen in place as he headed toward where I had been with empty racks for my chips.

"I assume none of you dare go in there," I said to the three gods standing beside me.

Laverne and Stan and Ben all nodded.

I had a hunch that was going to be the case. The more

power, the more that evil would push them away. I was barely able to just be near the table.

I turned to Stan. "I need Patty and Screamer."

Stan nodded and vanished.

"So we need to get that man away from that piece of the Relic, right?" I asked Ben. "To find out where he found it and if there are more pieces."

Ben nodded. "Critical."

"Will the evil be able to go through him to get to anyone here?" I asked.

This time both Laverne and Ben said no.

"And if we get him away from the Relic piece," I asked, "what can we do with it then?"

"Without the man close to it," Laverne said, "we can send it into the sun as we have done with all the other pieces. But we first must disconnect anyone attached to the piece, otherwise the evil flows back instead of being destroyed."

"And you can do that?" I asked.

Laverne nodded. "Given enough distance between the two, I can break the bond the piece has over the man."

"And it won't transfer to anyone else?"

"Not unless another person touches it," Ben said, and Laverne nodded.

A moment later Stan appeared with Patty and Screamer.

Patty had on her uniform from the front desk of the MGM Grand Hotel and her long brown hair pulled up and back. She looked as beautiful as ever.

Beside her Screamer looked as Screamer always did in his

jeans, long-sleeved shirt and short brown hair. Both of them were looking worried. I was sure Stan had told them nothing.

"Oh, oh," Patty said as she appeared, turning toward the table.

She could clearly feel it as well.

"What the hell is that?" Screamer asked, also turning toward the table across the poker room.

"Part of the Relic," I said.

Screamer looked puzzled, but Patty softly just shook her head. "I had hoped to go my entire life and never have to deal with another piece of that evil."

"All right," I said to my team. "It's going to take all three of us if we're going to go drag that guy away from that table and out here. Without breaking the time bubble."

Patty nodded and Screamer looked like he had about a thousand questions, but kept them to himself.

"Stan, Laverne, can you hold the bubble?"

"Got it," Stan said, nodding.

"The evil in that piece will not want you doing what you are going to attempt to do," Laverne said. "It will fight you."

"How?" I asked.

Laverne shook her head. "I do not know."

"You will need a magic-based shield," Ben said.

Now all of us turned to look at him. Both Stan and Laverne were looking as puzzled as I felt.

Ben nodded. "A magic-based shield is an old and almost lost art, but Poker Boy, I think you could do it, with help from Patty."

Ben turned to the table. "Feel the evil coming from that piece like waves of energy?"

I nodded. Once I had my warning powers cut down, I actually could sense the energy waves coming from the piece.

"Hold Patty's hand now," Ben said, "and focus about a foot in front of you both all the good energy you can master. Hold it there like a wall. Imagine it a wall. Patty, focus as much good and calming energy as you can into Poker Boy."

I could feel Patty's energy coming into me and I did as Ben had told me to do, building an imaginary wall with good energy in front of me, between all of us and that table.

Suddenly I could barely sense the evil. And I could almost see the shield shimmering in front of me.

"Stan," Laverne said, "you and I funnel him more energy."

Suddenly I could no longer feel the evil at all as energy poured through me from Stan and Laverne and Patty.

"Screamer, behind me," I said. "Let's go get that guy out of there."

I kept hold of Patty's hand and kept the image of the shimmering screen between me and that piece of metal sitting on the table.

The closer we got, the more I focused on the shield.

I could feel the evil in that piece pushing back, fighting to keep us away.

It felt like I was pushing a wide board against a river current, working it upstream.

We came in behind the guy frozen at the table. I did not

let go of Patty's hand, but with my free hand I took one side of the guy's chair and tipped it back while Screamer took the other side.

The energy coming from Laverne and Stan and Ben now increased as the energy from the evil fought us.

I felt like I was caught between two intense currents and that imaginary shield in front of me was all that was keeping us in place.

The evil in that piece of energy was very, very powerful.

We pulled, moving the guy back from the table, dragging the chair along the carpeted floor.

I wasn't sure how much longer I could hold up that imaginary shield, but I somehow did as we got the guy back away from the table and Ben and Stan came ducking in to help as we beat a full retreat, the frozen guy not even having a clue that he was being pulled away from the table in an instant of time.

We pulled the guy clear out onto the casino main floor.

I could almost not feel the energy from the evil, so I dropped the screen, panting.

"Ben," I said, looking at our newest team member, "will it be safe for us to go into the guy's mind and find where he found the piece?"

"At this distance it should be if we don't release the time bubble. But it wouldn't hurt to have the screen back up as well."

"Got the time bubble solid," Stan said, indicating the time bubble that kept us out of the normal flow of time.

I took a deep breath and could feel the energy coming back into me from Patty's grasp as I again imagined the screen between us and that piece of metal on the table.

Then Screamer touched me and I could feel all of us linked inside Screamer's head. It was such a familiar thing now, it didn't even bother me.

Keep that screen up, Screamer thought at me.

Then he touched the poor guy we had hauled away from the table.

I was right. He wasn't from around here. He was from a mountain town in Northern California, just south of the Oregon border. And he wasn't a poker player either. And he didn't have the five hundred to lose. He had been forced to sit at that table to find someone with magic. Clearly the evil entity in the piece had felt me sitting there and thought I would be an easy mark.

Screamer dug down into the guy's mind as I held the screen between all of us and the evil Relic piece.

I could see where the evil had taken over, the darkness in the guy, the unexplained actions, everything. Normally, he was a good man, but he had been controlled to go in search of magic.

Then the image became clear and I damn near let go of everything I was so shocked.

Patty thought clearly, *Oh, oh. Hold on.*

The guy had found the piece in an old mine in Northern California, just south of the Oregon boarder. He had dug down and ran into a cavern. And there in that underground cavern were many, many more pieces of the Relic. A vast number as far as I could see from the guy's mind.

Thousands at least.

If just one piece had caused Hitler, I could only imagine what all those pieces could do if let lose with magic in the world.

Screamer got the exact location of the cavern, then backed us out of the guy's head, then let go of me so the contact between the three of us was broken.

"Bad?" Laverne asked, looking worried.

"Really bad," I said, holding up the screen. "An entire cavern of pieces of the Relic."

"But he's the only one who knows about it," Patty said.

"I have the exact location," Screamer said.

"Stan, Ben, stay here," Laverne said. "Poker Boy, hold that screen up for as long as you can."

I nodded and Patty gripped my hand even tighter as Laverne, Screamer, and the poor miner from Northern California vanished, chair and all.

We all stood there like that for at least a minute. I was doing my best to hold that wall of good energy up between all of us and that piece of metal on the table.

Then suddenly there was a white light, very bright, that formed on the surface of the poker table and then vanished.

I could feel now that the screen I was holding up was no longer getting attacked from the other side.

A moment later Laverne appeared again with the guy in the chair.

"We broke the connection and that piece has been tossed into the sun, she said."

I sighed and dropped the shield I had just learned how to do, feeling the relief of the lack of energy drain.

And I realized I was suddenly very, very hungry.

"I got him," Stan said.

He touched the back of the chair and teleported the guy to his position at the table.

"What is happening with the cavern?" Patty asked a moment before I could.

"We're going to teleport them all into the sun," Laverne said. "After I broke the connection with the Relic, Screamer and I got the information from the man's head as well. They will all be gone within the next few minutes."

"That place was flat scary."

"We came very close to another major war with the Relic," Lady Luck said, nodding. "Great job once again, to all of you."

And then she turned to Ben. "It sure seems Poker Boy was correct. You are greatly needed on his team."

Ben smiled and I could see him gain energy. "It feels good to be needed."

He turned to me and said simply, "Thank you."

Then he vanished.

Lady Luck smiled at me once again. "Yes, thank you."

And she vanished.

I turned to Patty. "See you in about twenty minutes when you get off work?"

"Dinner is on me," Stan said. "Steaks. We'll meet in the lobby at the MGM in thirty minutes."

Then my boss looked at me.

"You got it?"

"I got it," I said and took back over the time bubble as he and Patty and Screamer vanished.

I moved back over to the table and tried to remember where I was standing when I took myself out of the time stream.

Then I let the time bubble go.

The sounds of the casino crashed in on me again. Amazing how loud a casino can be and how I only really notice it when the sounds are gone.

The guy who had the Relic suddenly looked around, clearly very puzzled.

I turned to James as he approached. "Rack that guy's chips back up first. He doesn't belong at this table."

James looked puzzled, but went around and did as I suggested as the guy stood, clearly very, very puzzled and with only a fuzzy memory of how he had got seated in a poker game four hundred miles from his home.

"Better call your wife," I said to him, smiling and sending him a calming influence. "She's going to be worried."

James handed him his chips.

"Help him cash those out," I said to James. "I'll rack my own."

Then I handed James a twenty-five dollar chip and he nodded, leading the guy from the table.

"What just happened?" Carl the dealer asked, glancing back at the guy walking away as I stared racking up my winnings for the night.

"Besides stopping an alien invasion and saving the world from being taken over by great evil, not much."

Carl laughed, shaking his head as I took my chips. I tossed Carl a twenty-five dollar chip as a tip and went to the coat tree and got the guy's coat and took it across the room to him.

Sometimes telling the truth seemed funny.

Even when it wasn't.

A Desert Shot

Chapter One

Strangely enough, as a superhero, I seldom see a body. It happens, sure, but rarely. If someone gets to the body state, I figured I failed in my Poker Boy superhero duties.

The body on the hard desert dirt in front of me hadn't been anyone I had known. The body had been out in the hot sun long enough that it had started to get ripe-smelling. I had a hunch the ripe odor would turn real sour real quick if this guy didn't get moved out of the sun sooner rather than later.

The body had on a light tan golf shirt, golf shoes, matching tan golf slacks, and a tan golf glove. The tan sort of washed out his already really white skin. Not a good choice of color for his last day on the planet.

Of course, I had on my black leather jacket and black

fedora-like hat standing in the hot desert sun, so I wasn't one to give fashion advice.

From what I could figure, the dead guy had been about forty with a slight gut and about forty extra pounds. No telling what killed him. No blood stained the bland clothing in any place I could see.

And I sure wasn't touching the body to move it. That would be up to the police.

However, I did find it odd that there wasn't a golf course within ten miles of this spot to the north of Las Vegas. In fact, there wasn't much of anything near this spot but sagebrush and rocks and more than likely a large herd of rattlesnakes. Or bunch of rattlesnakes, or group, or whatever a mass of nasty, mean, and deadly snakes are called.

About a mile to the east, I could hear faint freeway noise of trucks and cars with no mufflers, but otherwise the desert blanketed the dead guy with silence and a lot of heat.

Way too much heat for a leather jacket.

Stan, the God of Poker, had brought me to this spot next to this dead guy with the balding head and blank, dead stare in dark eyes. So I turned to Stan who stood there in his dark slacks, tan button-down sweater, and loafers and asked the most logical question I could think to ask after being surprised by teleporting from a comfortable diner booth in my office to a spot next to a body.

"Think maybe we should call the police?"

Stan took us out of time, which had the effect of cutting off the freeway sounds and wind that was keeping the guy's ripening smell away. He motioned that I should follow him and we moved about fifty steps away from the bland dead guy, staying inside the time bubble the entire time.

"Thank you," I said. "So what are we doing here? And who's the dead guy?"

"Not a clue," Stan said. "And I honestly don't know why we're here."

Now that made me turn my attention from the now distant dead body and look directly at my boss, the God of Poker.

He shrugged, actually looking puzzled.

"So you didn't pluck me from that hamburger and vanilla shake in my office?"

"I did not," he said, shaking his head.

"Now I'm worried," I said.

"Yeah," my boss said, agreeing.

"Stop fretting," a voice said from behind us. "I brought you here."

Stan and I both spun around to look down at a short man in dark brown golf slacks, a white golf shirt, a golf hat with a Dunes logo on it, and a brown golf glove. His face was almost round and clearly he had spent far, far too much time in the sun without enough sunscreen. I could barely see his green eyes through the bright red folds of skin on his cheeks that threatened to crawl up and cover his bushy eyebrows at any moment.

I glanced at Stan who had dropped all pretenses of a poker face and was looking as puzzled as I felt. The guy clearly had a lot of magic since he had walked right into the time bubble Stan had around us.

"Laverne," Stan said. "A little help?"

Lady Luck herself appeared next to Stan facing the little golfer.

She frowned.

I can say clearly as a poker player that when Lady Luck frowns, bad things happen.

She glanced over at the body lying on the hard ground of the desert, then back at Stan and me.

The little golfer bowed slightly to her, the smile on his face making the sunburn seem brighter. With the smile, his eyes sunk farther into the rolls of red flesh.

"Work with him," she said to Stan, shaking her head. "He obviously needs your help. You too, Poker Boy. Shouldn't take too long."

She looked at me and I nodded, damn near the only thing a sane person could do when commanded to do something by Lady Luck herself.

Then she vanished.

"I love her," the little golfer said, smiling at me. "Don't you just love her? A little brisk at times, but still a real charmer. Don't you think?"

I said nothing. There wasn't enough money on the planet to get me to say a word about Lady Luck.

"So who are you and what do you want?" Stan asked, his voice cold and low.

The little golfer smiled and bowed slightly, tipping his golf hat just a slight touch. "I'm Benny Douglas, the world's greatest detective, at your service."

I had no idea who he was. Not clue one. Or what area he was a god in.

But Stan seemed to know him and he sighed and nodded. "Your reputation precedes you."

"I hope like the sweet smell of a dozen roses for a beautiful woman on a first date," Benny said.

"Whatever," Stan said.

Oh, wow, Stan didn't much like this guy and was not bothering to hide the fact.

"So what do you need us for?" I asked.

"To help me solve poor Dan's murder, of course," Benny said, indicating the body that wasn't decaying or smelling at the moment because Stan was holding us in a time bubble outside of the flow of time.

I decided right then that I didn't much like this short little golfer who called himself a detective. So I figured a really, really stupid question might just get under his skin a little.

"So who killed Dan?" I asked, expecting him to give me nothing more than a dirty look.

Benny actually sighed at my seemingly stupid question. "Sadly, I think I might have. But I need you both to help me prove that I didn't. And find out what really killed him."

I stared at the short detective. That was not at all the answer I had expected.

Chapter Two

"Time to call the police," I said, turning to my boss. "Let them figure it out."

"Almost starting to agree with you," Stan said, staring at Benny.

Around us the silence in the time bubble seemed to almost match the look of the empty desert.

Benny held up his hands for us to stop. "Look, let me explain what happened and we can go from there, all right? I trust you two, heard you've helped a lot of people, figured you could help me some on this. And remember Laverne told you to help me and don't you both work for that fine lady?"

I stood there, saying nothing. I wanted to say, "Asking for help would have been nice." But I said nothing instead.

Stan did the same.

After a moment Benny caught the clue and started talking even faster than before, which I was surprised was possible.

"Me and Dan there were on the third hole and we were partnered up in a match against Goldenburg and his assistant Tammy. She's a sweet one, that Tammy, fills out those golf shorts real nice if you get my drift, and can hit a driver farther than the rest of us without even messing up her long brown hair."

"Are you talking about Goldenburg, the God of Magic and Illusion?" Stan asked.

Benny nodded like his chin was on a spring on his chest and some kid had ahold of the string and was pulling it. "Sure, who else?"

Stan just stared at Benny.

I decided to just keep quiet and ask who Goldenburg was when I really needed to know.

"So which team was winning?" Stan asked.

"We were," Benny said. "Two up and about to take the third hole as well. Goldenburg can't hit an iron to save his life, and Tammy, bless those tight shorts, can't putt, but it sure is fun to watch her try, if you get my drift."

"The bet?" Stan asked.

"We win," Benny said, "Tammy works for me for a month trying to get a hundred years of paperwork in my office filed," Benny said. "You know how it goes, a fella gets behind and then there's never enough time to get all the basic stuff done and besides, watching Tammy around the office for a month sure couldn't hurt a guy, if you get my drift."

I bit my lip to not say anything. I bit it hard. Patty Ledgerwood, my girlfriend and sidekick says I look cute when I do that. But cute or not, at least it kept me from spouting out something that would derail Stan's questions.

"If you lose?" Stan asked.

"I wash dishes in Dan's restaurant down off The Strip for a month to help pay for a month's worth of dinners Goldenburg and Tammy were going to eat there."

Benny shook his head and looked over at Dan's body. "We weren't going to lose, no way. Until this."

"So how did you kill your own golfing partner?" I asked.

Benny just shook his head. "He missed his second shot on the third hole and I might have made some comment about him being a dead weight or something like that and when I got done putting my club back in my bag he was gone."

"And then what happened?" Stan asked

Benny shrugged. "We looked for him all over, but after five minutes Goldenburg said we had looked long enough and the rules of golf said we had to move on."

"Pretty sure that rule applies to lost golf balls, not partners," Stan said.

I again kept my mouth shut since I knew nothing at all about golf. It wouldn't have surprised me, though, to know that there was a rule that you could only look for a lost partner for five minutes before moving on. Golf seemed that odd to me.

"I told them to keep going and I would search for Dan," Benny said. "I traced him here and that's when I got you two because, honestly, I didn't know what to think and all this seems just odd to me, being a detective and all, but I sure can't trust my own gut on this one."

"So what's your gut telling you?" I asked Benny.

"That this is some sort of Goldenburg trick on me to get free dinners for a month at Dan's place and I wouldn't be surprised that even with Dan dead, Goldenburg will still collect after he wins."

Suddenly something that had been dinging in the back of my mind sort of dinged again, only slightly louder, like a timer on a microwave going off.

"What did Dan get if you two won?"

Benny looked at me and opened his mouth and then shut it. The little golfer detective was speechless for the first time since he pulled us to this body.

Stan laughed. "Seems like Dan only won with you washing dishes for a month."

"So you saying him dying is a trick to get me to wash dishes at his place? I mean, not a very logical plan for a long-term business model."

"Is he really dead?" I asked Benny. I hadn't been able to get much of a read on Benny up until that question. I seldom did on the more powerful gods, but suddenly I could feel Benny being very uncertain and confused.

"Smelled dead," Benny said.

"How about you go check him out to be sure," Stan said, releasing the time bubble.

The wind snapped against my skin once again and the

distant sounds of trucks on the freeway echoed over the sagebrush.

Benny shook his head slowly back and forth. "Never touched a dead body before and you know, maybe you're right, maybe we should be calling the police and all that."

"Go roll him over, see if he really is dead," Stan said, his boss voice in full command.

I had a hunch that Dan was far from dead.

Benny took a deep breath and then in his brown golf shoes headed across the hard desert ground toward the body.

If nothing else, this was going to be entertaining watching him sneak up on his dead golfing partner.

Chapter Three

Benny finally reached the body and I could tell he had been holding his breath the entire time since he swayed slightly like he was about to pass out.

He gently reached down to roll Dan over and the body vanished, leaving only the carcass of a very dead coyote that clearly had been picked over by birds and other desert animals and was the source of the ripe smell.

Dan's body had been only an illusion, made very real by the smell.

Nice trick.

A good illusion is always in the details and smell was the detail that made this one.

Benny jumped back and instantly teleported to a spot back in front of us. His face was bright red, his green eyes intense and clearly angry.

"Where the hell did Dan's body go? Did you two do that? Did Laverne? Who would take Dan's body? We need to go to the police. Body theft is a serious crime."

"As if murder isn't," I said, shaking my head.

"There was no body," Stan said.

I was having trouble understanding that Stan needed to even explain that to Benny.

"No body, no murder?" Benny asked, clearly puzzled.

The little golfer who claimed to be the world's best detective wasn't really carrying a full bag of clubs when it came to deductive reasoning.

"An illusion," I said. "You said Goldenburg was the God of Magic, right?"

Benny nodded, slowly starting to understand.

I turned to Stan. "To project an illusion like that, wouldn't Dan have to be involved?"

"More than likely," Stan said. "At least at some point. Don't blame Dan, though, since he only got something if they lost."

"So, Benny," I asked our little golfing detective, "what hole are they on and is Dan with them?"

Benny seemed to stare off into the distance for a moment, then grow even redder in his face, something I didn't think was possible.

"They are on the sixth hole and Dan's as healthy as he gets, which isn't going very far since last year he had two bypass surgeries and has a blood sugar level that would kill a honey bee."

Benny kept staring off into the distance. "I bet we're now two holes down because I was gone and Dan can't play a lick of golf and more than likely has fallen down a few times staring at Tammy's shorts, not that I blame him for that, if you get my drift."

Benny glanced up at me and then at Stan. "So you two are telling me that I didn't accidently kill Dan, that's really him playing golf with Goldenburg?"

Stan and I both nodded.

"And that Dan was helping Goldenburg trick me so that they could win the match and I would end up doing dishes for a month in his place?"

Stan and I again both nodded.

"Wow, you guys are as good as everyone says you are," Benny said. "I never would have figured that out on my own."

I almost said that I had guessed that, but again did the cute thing and bit my lip.

"What are you going to do when you rejoin them?" Stan asked.

"Nothing," Benny said. "Just going on as if nothing had happened and win the match and get Tammy and those great shorts of hers to help me get my office straightened out. I really should have hired someone fifty years ago, but you know how it goes when a fella gets busy."

Stan and I both stood there in the wind of the desert and said nothing. Lady Luck had been right. This hadn't taken very long at all.

"I owe you two," Benny said, smiling, his green eyes lost in the rolls of red flesh on his cheeks. "You solved the murder and saved my life."

"There was no murder, Benny," Stan said.

"Yeah, whatever," Benny said and tipped his golf hat and vanished.

I turned to Stan. "How about I buy you lunch and you tell me who that guy really is."

"The world's greatest detective," Stan said, keeping a perfect poker face. "He told you."

"If he's the world's greatest detective, then I'm Sherlock Holmes."

"You can't be," Stan said.

"And why not?"

"Because Sherlock Holmes is a fictional character."

"And Benny isn't fictional, at least in his own mind?"

"No, he's the world's greatest detective as he said."

"It's going to be one of those lunchtime conversations, isn't it?" I asked.

Stan just smiled and jumped us away from the dead coyote and hot sun and sagebrush and back to my office.

I never did find out if Benny ended up winning the services of Tammy for a month. And the first time I used the phrase "...if you get my drift" around Patty, she made me swear to never use it again.

It seemed she also had met Benny at some point in the past.

THE GODS AREN'T FUNNY

THE GODS AREN'T FUNNY

I was starting to really dread Christmas Eve.

I mean, do you blame me? Two Christmas Eves ago my old girlfriend, Julie Downer, came to me for help. Then she didn't like my suggestions about what to do, even though I offered to pay for her new boob job. Eventually she ended up getting her breasts sucked out through her ass by the Silicon Suckers, which needless to say, killed her.

Makes me shudder just to think about it.

And then last year short Bob showed up in the poker room, knowing he was going to die in the morning, and wanting to leave with ten thousand so that he could go out of the world exactly as he had come in: Dead Even.

As a poker player, I understood his desire, but his poker playing ability sucked, right along with his bad temper. I ended up just giving him the ten big ones on a sham bet. He died right when he said he would.

So do you blame me for being a little spooked? Two years in a row someone who had come to me for help on Christmas Eve had died. And neither of them I could have done anything about, even though during the last year I had wondered if I could have.

Guilt trips are often my strong suit, which I understand from other super heroes, is one of our professional hazards. We help fifty people, but it's the one we can't help that haunts us. I had two on two successive years that I couldn't save. I was in guilt trip heaven.

Now, it was Christmas Eve morning again. So far no one had shown up, and I was determined to forget Bob and Julie and just have my normal Christmas Eve.

The day dawned bright, the air crisp, the light snow not bothering anyone getting to Spirit Winds Casino. My plan for this Christmas Eve was the same as I had done for the last dozen or so holidays, at least the ones people didn't die around me.

I would go over to the Casino in the early evening, and get into a poker game with the rest of the non-family poker players.

Many poker players don't have family, and many of us like it that way, so I had little worries that there wouldn't be a game.

I would play until some time in the morning, go home and get some sleep, and be back in the poker room after a turkey dinner in the buffet. If I timed it right, I would be there for the really good games that always started later Christmas Day.

An aside. A really good game to a professional poker player like myself is when there are a bunch of people with a lot of money and very little skill. Those kinds were there to have fun, and I bless them for their goals. I did everything in my power to have fun right along with them as I took their money. Late Christmas Day seemed to have an extra number of these types showing up, done with their family obligations and ready to have some fun.

I loved my holiday schedule, I loved the sameness of it year after year, I loved not having to put up a tree or buy anyone presents or hang stupid lights on my gutters. I just did my thing and enjoyed it. So even though I was a super hero, sworn to help those I could help, I didn't want anyone to come asking for help this Christmas. My track record just wasn't good.

I'd even lost a dog the first year, and that was the only time in my memory of being Poker Boy, super hero who helps people and saves dogs, that I had ever lost a dog. Other people had died when they didn't take my advice, which wasn't my fault. And there really hadn't been anything I could have done to stop Bob's massive heart attack last year. I could live with that, but I hated not being able to save dogs.

I had almost made it to the poker room when I saw her. She was sitting on a bench near the front door of the casino, her back to the window, her posture straight, her eyes focused on the people who went past, watching every move, clearly searching for something or someone.

She had longish blonde hair, a body that looked tanned and in good shape, and she definitely had her proportions in order. She was also at least fifteen years younger than me.

So sue me, I'm human underneath all the super hero stuff. I can look at a good-looking woman, even though a women like the one sitting there never looked back.

The she looked up at me, directly at me, actually seeing me, and I was struck by her deep, blue eyes.

She smiled and I was pulled by her wonderful, friendly smile.

She patted the bench beside her and I knew at once I was hooked, not by the woman's charms, or good looks, or great, perfectly proportioned body, but by some power even greater than my Poker Boy casino-fed powers.

I moved over, walking like a stiff-legged zombie in a bad movie, and sat beside her as if I didn't have an ounce of control over my body. And when a super hero loses control of his body, that's a very bad sign.

An aside. I have been with my share of beautiful women over the years who have made me lose control of all, or part, of my body, and this is not what had just happened. This was no little head controlling the big head. This was magic or super power or something besides womanly charms, although I must admit, womanly charms often act like a super power on me. Just not this time.

When I was seated, I felt the control over whatever had

made me do the monster walk loosen, and then vanish, like heat coming from an oven when you open the door and try to look in too fast. My eyes fogged for an instant, I felt flush, and then it was gone.

"Wow, that was pretty good," I said. "You use that power for helping others, or just making people walk funny?"

She laughed, the sound high and just a trifle shrill, but she was so good-looking, and had such perfect skin on her perfectly proportioned body, I didn't much care about a slightly-off laugh.

"No," she said, "I'm no super hero like you, Poker Boy."

My instant reaction was <u>Shit! She knew my name!</u>

But she went on talking before those words came out of my mouth.

"Dave gave me that power," she said, "to make sure I got your attention when I found you. I could only use it the one time."

"Dave?" I asked, actually getting the word out of my suddenly dry mouth. My stomach was twisting like I had just had two big polish dogs and forgot to take an antacid. There was only one Dave I knew who could give super powers away like they were quarters.

"Dave," she said, nodding. "I was sitting in his office just yesterday."

For a moment the word "Dave" echoed a little around the lobby of the casino like she had shouted it into a deep canyon.

An aside. In my world there are a number of what are called Gambling Gods. My super power as Poker Boy, I am sure, comes directly from the Gambling Gods. Now these gods are more like what I would have imagined the old Greek gods were like. And there is a very clear hierarchy in the Gambling Gods' world.

The hierarchy is set up just like a casino management. In fact, there's a major discussion about whether the gods just recently patterned their world on how super casinos were run, or if casinos patterned their management after how the gods have always been.

I actually think the Gambling Gods have always had the same management system, and modern super casinos just followed along naturally. Or not so naturally, but that's only my opinion, and I really don't know for sure.

At the top of this system is the General Manager. The General Manager is the most powerful, can stomp on other gods like they were ants, and pretty much controls the nature of the world behind the normal world that most people see.

Below the General Manager comes the Head of Casino Operations, then the Head of Hotel Operations. Below them are all the directors, such as Director of Security, Director of Food and Beverage, Director of Entertainment, and so on. And below that group are the Managers, such as the Keno Manager and Poker Room Manager.

The gods below those didn't much count, and I figured I had as much power as Poker Boy as many of the lower level gods, like Pit Bosses and Shift Supervisors. But they are still considered gods in the realm of things, and I am only a super hero, so what do I know. I certainly have no plan on putting my powers up against any of them.

Now this woman had just finished telling me she had talked to Dave, had been in Dave's office, and had gotten the power trick to get me to sit down from Dave.

To say I was stunned would be an understatement. Dave was the General Manager, the top of the top, the man with the big power.

You didn't bow to Dave, or worship him, but you certainly didn't mess with Dave, or make him angry. I honestly hoped I would never even meet Dave. I figured it was just safer that way.

Now Dave had sent this good-looking woman to me.

Up until this moment, I wasn't even sure if the General Manager of everything even knew I existed.

I desperately wanted to ask her what Dave's office looked like, what Dave looked like for that matter, but somehow I refrained from being a God geek and asked the most intelligent question I could think of.

"Dave sent you to me, huh? It must be really important."

Duh. Dumb-ass question. This was not getting off to a good start.

"I think it is," she said. "My name is Audrey Koch. Can I buy you a drink and tell you about it?"

Here was a beautiful woman asking to buy me a drink on Christmas Eve, and I was scared more than I have been in years.

"Buy me a Diet Coke" I said, keeping my voice level and

my poker face on. Thank god I was a poker player and I could do that under stressful situations. "I'll be glad to listen."

"Great," she said, standing up quickly like the bench had an ejection button.

I got up a little more slowly, making sure that all the Come-and-sit-beside-me spell was gone. It was, and two minutes later we were in the bar.

The place had twenty tables and a big screen t.v. Only one other couple sat against the far wall, so we took a table in front of the window looking out at the people headed from the hotel to the casino.

Audrey ordered an eggnog drink that sounded like it could cause diabetes all by itself, and I stuck with my original plan. I didn't want any alcohol because I still held out hope of getting to the poker table tonight. But with Dave sticking his all-powerful nose into my Christmas Eve, that hope was fading quickly.

"Here's my problem," Audrey said, getting right to the point. She looked me right in the eye and with the most serious of expression on her face said, "I need to get laid. And it has to happen in the next four hours and ten minutes."

She actually looked at her watch as she said that second sentence.

I glanced at my watch as well. Seven-fifty. Four hours and ten minutes until Christmas.

She wanted to get laid on Christmas Eve. Why?

I must have heard her wrong. That couldn't be the big

problem. The General Manager of the Big Casino couldn't be pimping me to some woman. It wasn't possible.

Besides, this woman could get just about any man she blinked at.

"Would you repeat that?" I asked.

She laughed, the sound echoing through the almost empty bar. Again the laugh was just a little off, but the wonderful blue eyes and the perfect smile made me not care at all.

"I need to have sex before midnight with a super hero. And Dave thought you would be the best choice for me."

"Oh, Dave thought I would, huh?"

She nodded, smiling. "And I agree. You're older than I usually like in men, but you're cute."

Okay, I'm a poker player, a guy who is usually in complete control of his emotions, yet right at that moment I didn't have a clue if I should feel angry, excited, flattered, or insulted. I was being pimped by the big guy in the Executive Suite to a young, very attractive woman. There had to be something I was missing, and I needed to resort to my super powers to find out.

I turned on my Tell-Me-No-Lies Super Power and stared directly at her.

An aside. I used to call this power my Empathy Super Power, but that never seemed to fit, so this year I finally renamed it.

"Why do you need to sleep with a super hero before Christmas Day?" I asked, directing all my power at her.

No person could resist me.

She resisted.

But no person could resist me.

She still resisted, bouncing my super power away like it was water on a freshly waxed car.

Then she blushed.

"Dave said you might try to get the truth out of me," she said. "He's blocked all your powers from working on me."

Then she shrugged and smiled. "Sorry."

I stopped focusing my useless power and sat back. What good was a super hero with his super powers not working? I pushed that thought away, and all thoughts of feeling sorry for myself, and directed my attention to her.

"You're not going to tell me why you want to sleep with me inside this time frame, are you?"

"I can't," she said, the look on her face deadly serious.

I sat there thinking while the waitress served our drinks and took Audry's money. I could only come up with a couple of reasons for this strange request.

First, the General Manager was rewarding me for all my good deeds over the years. But that didn't seem to be Dave's style. And this kind of reward certainly wasn't mine either.

Second, this was a bet. Bets in the Gambling God's world were every day things. Someone might have bet I would sleep with this woman before Christmas Day, giving up my evening of poker for sex. And Dave was in on the bet in some fashion.

I could think of no other reason this woman needed to sleep with a super hero this evening, before midnight.

None.

And if there was a reason, she should be able to tell me. Only things like bets made silly rules like not telling.

So it had to be a bet.

And I was just a pawn in the bet. Nothing more. But did I want to play poker tonight and let one side win the bet, or sleep with a beautiful, young woman, and let the other side win?

Actually, that was a tough choice for a professional poker player at my age. At twenty-nine, there would be no thought. The little head would have controlled the decision and thirty minutes later I'd be looking at this young woman's nude body.

But at forty-nine, sleeping with a woman always brought many side affects. I don't mean this to sound like I don't have relationships. I do. Just not ones that started in Dave's office and brought me into the picture doing a zombie walk. Thinking back, not one of my long-term relationships with women have started that way, and I doubted this would either.

My little voice told me there was still something I was missing.

An aside. My little voice isn't a super power, but it saves me more often than my powers do.

"Okay," I said, facing her as she sipped on her sugar-drink. "You want to sleep with a super hero before midnight, but you're not going to tell me why. Am I right?"

She nodded, her beautiful eyes staring at me.

"And I'm the super hero that Dave sort of picked out of a hat for you, right?"

This time she nodded a little slower. From what I could tell, that wasn't the complete truth, but I was getting close.

"You didn't even know I existed before Dave mentioned my name, did you?"

She shook her head this time, still saying nothing.

So I was just a convenient super hero, doing nothing on Christmas Eve but playing poker. This was making me a little angry, I had to admit.

"And I assume this is what you really look like, that you don't have AIDs, and you don't want to get pregnant."

"This is what I really look like," she said, spreading her arms, which gave me a clear view of her assets just above the table, "No magic, no nothing. I don't have any diseases, and I will never have kids."

"Yet right now you want to check into a hotel room and have sex with me?"

"I already have a room," she said, smiling at me.

Damn, if this woman was just a half-an-ounce less beautiful, had a fraction less fantastic smile, and didn't have such perfect skin, I wouldn't be having any problem. I'd be telling her it was nice meeting her and move on to the poker room.

But it was hard for any mortal man, super hero or not, to turn down an offer of sex from a goddess-like woman.

Then I realized what word had gone through my head. <u>Goddess.</u>

No wonder she had access to Dave. This woman was one of the Gambling Gods. Oh, shit! Now what should I do?

Sleeping with a Gambling God can only cause trouble. I've heard that a dozen times over the years.

But not sleeping with a Gambling God in this situation could cause even more troubles. Again I needed more information.

And I had always felt the best way to get information was directly.

"Can you tell me more about yourself?" I asked, sipping on my diet coke. "For example, I know you're one of the gods. Which position do you hold?"

Her face turned white and she tried to cover it quickly by bending forward and taking another sip of her drink. I'm a poker player. I can read expressions like other people read books. I knew for a fact I had hit the right answer with my little fishing question.

Finally she looked up at me. "How did you know? And without your super powers?"

"You're dealing with a poker player. How would I not know?"

She nodded, taking that in. Finally she said, "I guess I can tell you. I'm the Keno Manager."

"So Audry isn't your real name," I said. "You're Betty."

I had made it a habit of following all the main and lower gods, and who left, who got moved, who moved up or down, and so on. I was a poker player and a super hero. It was just part of my super hero job.

I reached across the table, hand extended. She took my hand and I shook hers, saying, "Nice meeting you, Betty."

"Nice to meet you as well, Poker Boy," she said, smiling, those teeth perfect in the bar light.

So now that I knew who she really was, there were only two options available as to why she was doing what she was doing. First, it was a bet as I had figured before.

But the second reason felt to be the more likely prospect. Betty wanted to move either up, or sideways, in her job status in the Gambling God Big Casino.

Suddenly I knew the answer. Dave was involved, therefore this wasn't a bet. This was an audition.

Betty was trying to move over to Poker Room manager and take Stan's job. And Dave must have figured that if she understood a major poker player enough to get him to sleep with her instead of playing poker, she might get the job.

Now twice over the last few years I had met Stan, both times in the middle of adventures. Usually the Gambling Gods didn't get involved in my adventures, and I doubted they even paid much attention most of the time.

But I liked Stan. He treated me fairly. I wasn't so sure yet that I liked Betty. Granted, any normal, heterosexual man would want to sleep with her, but that aside, I didn't have a good feeling about her.

And she had clearly let me surprise her as well. No one surprised Stan. And he seemed to understand poker players.

Betty clearly understood sex. And since Keno had the worst odds of any game in a casino except the Big Wheel, she understood suckers. And she was playing me as one during this entire exchange.

Poker Players hated being played as suckers, even though the payout was sex with a goddess. It still wasn't worth it.

I took a sip out of my drink and leaned forward over the table. "Betty, you are a stunningly beautiful goddess."

"Well, thank you," she said, beaming that beaming smile at me.

"And I think you will make great middle management in the Big Casino."

"I hear a but coming," she said, her smile now gone.

"But I don't think you'd make a good Poker Room Manager. You're going to have to find another way to move up."

She sat there staring at me for a moment, her mouth slightly open. Clearly I had hit the nail right on the head. I had read her reasons and motives like I read a mid-level poker player.

"Dave told me I wouldn't be able to fool you," she said. "But I don't understand how you knew without your super powers. Did Stan tell you?"

"No one told me," I said. "I'm a poker player. Knowing people and understanding why they do what they do is my job, and how I make my living. And I'm very good at my job."

She nodded. "Dave told me that if I didn't understand poker players, I could never have the job. Clearly I don't. At least not yet. You want to give me a private lesson?"

She smiled such a seductive smile, I thought the glass in my hand might melt. Yet somehow I managed to hold on.

"Sorry," I said. "I hope you don't hold this against me." Actually, I hoped that a lot, but I figured that since I helped Stan keep his job, Stan was going to help me as well if I needed protection from Betty.

"No hard feelings," she said, still smiling, only with the seductive part dropped. "But tell me, how would I have gotten you into bed if I had known poker players."

"Just play good cards," I said, giving her the same advice I gave any beginning poker player. "And never get in the way of a big game."

She nodded. "And tonight's a big game for you?"

"It is," I said. I had really been looking forward to my Christmas poker ritual, especially after the last two years.

She laughed softly, and stood, extending her beautiful, perfect-skinned hand. "Well, Poker Boy, it certainly has been an education meeting you. I'm sorry we're not going have that roll in the sheets."

"Not half as sorry as I am," I said, taking her hand and holding it.

Her off-kilter laugh echoed through the mostly empty restaurant as she faded away, leaving me with my hand extended into mid-air.

I turned and headed for the poker room. No one had died on me yet on this Christmas Eve. And I kept Stan's job for him, which had to be worth a little. So far, so good.

And I hadn't even played a hand of cards yet.

The 13th Floor Problem

CHAPTER ONE

As a professional poker player, I don't have any superstitions. Not a one. I don't believe that if I won a tournament with one sock inside out, that I needed to always wear one sock inside out for good luck. I know for a fact that Lady Luck, actually named Laverne, paid no attention at all to how my socks were worn, or if I threw salt over my shoulder, or if I walked under a ladder.

She was just too busy. Now don't take me wrong, I wouldn't want to cross her, but she just wasn't the type to pay attention to the small stuff.

In life and in poker, I have had my fair share of good luck and bad luck, even though as Poker Boy, I know Lady Luck likes me, and my team. In fact, one of her four daughters, Terri, the Queen of Clubs, has just joined my team of superheroes.

My team works to save the world when it needs saving and it is often Lady Luck who gives us the assignments.

As it happened, just luck or coincidence or whatever, most of my team was having lunch in my office when we learned about what we came to call "The 13ᵗʰ Floor Problem."

My office, actually it's my team's office, but everyone calls it my office, floats about five hundred feet above the top floor of MGM Grand Hotel and Casino. It has windows on all four sides, floor-to-ceiling, with a view that was worth more than I wanted to ever imagine.

How it stayed in position was beyond me, even though Stan said I was the one who put it there and kept it there. As far as I was concerned, it stayed in place by some sort of magic I didn't understand. There were a lot of things in the world of gods and superheroes that I didn't understand and how my office worked was one of those things.

The office was, of course, invisible, and, as Stan said, out of phase with the real world so that if a plane hit it, the plane would pass right through. I'm sure if that happened, it would give everyone in the office a heart attack. The last thing I wanted was a plane passing through me.

But the office did have a wonderful view of the Strip and the airport and the entire city around it. Patty Ledgerwood (aka Front Desk Girl and my girlfriend and sidekick) and I often came up here at night and sat together and watched the stars and the planes landing and the cars on the Strip and all the bright lights spread out below us. As I said, a view worth more than I can imagine.

I had decorated the office so it looked like an exact replica of the 1960's diner booth the team used to meet in. The Diner, as the place is called, is in the downtown Vegas area on a side street a block from the Horseshoe Casino and Hotel.

Just as in the Diner downtown, this booth had slick, red seats on three sides. I had added wooden chairs that could be pulled up to the end of the booth and a couple tall, tree-like plants behind the booth to give the place a little less cold feel.

The booth filled most of the room and could seat eight in a pinch.

There were only three ways to get up to the office. I had put a door leading to Patti's apartment and another door leading to the Diner in downtown Vegas. You step through and you were instantly in the other place. Otherwise you had to teleport.

I could teleport, but besides Stan, the God of Poker and my boss, I was the only one on the team who could. Everyone else either hitched a ride here with me or Stan or used the door from the Diner.

I was told it was rare that a lowly superhero like me could teleport. Or step between instants of time. But I had learned how to do both. I figured if I could learn it, so could other superheroes, like my girlfriend, Patty. She was a superhero working in hotel hospitality area of the Gods.

She was willing to learn, so we had worked on it a few times, so far without luck. But we had time and one of Patty's super-hero traits was extreme patience. She had to have that to put up with me at times. I was a professional poker player, after all.

It had become a habit for the team to have lunch together in my office around the big booth at one in the afternoon. We all liked the view and the companionship. Sometimes being a superhero could get lonely, at least that's what others told me. As a poker player, I always had people around me. It was part of the job.

And I was lucky enough to be tangled up with Patty.

Screamer and his wife, Terri, were sitting at the table working on burgers and vanilla shakes that Madge from the Diner had brought up. Having the great food and milkshakes from the Diner in downtown Vegas just a step through a door away was a great benefit.

Screamer had been a member of the team since we started. He was a superhero working with the police and could, with a touch, connect minds and be inside another person's mind. He got his nickname Screamer from making hardened crimi-nals scream in fear from the images he put in their heads.

Terri was Lady Luck's daughter and a superhero in the beverage side of things. She and Screamer had been separated for a number of years while he got his newly-acquired brain-reading powers under control. Now that they had worked out a way to be together, they never seemed to be apart.

Patty worked at the MGM Grand front desk and was on lunch break, so she still had on her front desk outfit and her long, brown hair pulled back tight. She nibbled at a salad while I worked at a cheeseburger with a huge basket of fries. I had switched away from my standard vanilla milkshake today for a cherry Diet Coke. Patty was mixing my fries with her salad, taking a bite of lettuce, then a fry.

Stan, the God of Poker, and my boss, also had a cheeseburger. He had on his standard tan slacks, tan shirt, and tan vest. He was the most nondescript man I had ever met. You could almost look right at him and not notice him. That made him downright scary on a poker table.

I had just taken a huge bite of my cheeseburger when Laverne, Lady Luck herself, appeared, pulled up a chair, sat at the booth, and grabbed one of my fries. Between her and Patty, I was going to be lucky to get any of them.

Laverne wore her normal gray silk business pants suit and had her hair pulled back tight, giving her face a stark beauty and sternness. She just radiated power and toughness.

And not once being around her did I fail to get nervous. Having Lady Luck herself just come to have lunch with you was a stunning thing I would never get over.

"Hey, Mom," Terri said, working at her hamburger and leaning against Screamer.

I managed to get most of the ketchup off my chin and nodded to her. Stan just kept working on his cheeseburger.

Madge appeared out of the door from the diner and smiled at Laverne. "Anything I can get for you?"

Madge was the waitress and the owner of the Diner downtown. She was also a superhero in the food and beverage industry and seemed to have been around the world of the gods for a very long time. She was fairly short and clearly over-weight and she always wore a dress far, far too tight and too short for someone her size. She had a gruff way about her, but was always willing to help out the team where she could. She knew everyone, which had helped a few times on different assignments we had tackled.

Laverne shook her head. "Thanks, Madge, but we have a problem we need to get started on."

I swallowed the last of the bite of my cheeseburger I had been chewing on and pushed the rest away. When Laverne came looking for us like this, it meant eating was going to take a back seat very quickly.

Besides, my stomach was already twisting from my sense of looming danger, so putting more food down there wasn't a good idea at the moment.

"What's happening?" Stan asked, then took another bite of his cheeseburger.

"All the thirteenth floors are vanishing," Laverne said, as if she said a statement like that every day.

Then she took another fry.

"No building or hotel in this city has a thirteenth floor," Terri said, looking puzzled.

"Floor Twelve B or the Fourteenth Floor, whatever they are called," Laverne said, shrugging. "They are all vanishing. They will still be there, so no building is going to fall down, but the floors will become totally invisible by midnight."

"The Magician is back," Madge said, shaking her head and sighing in a way I had never heard before.

"Maybe," Laverne said, taking one more fry. She gave me that serious stare that scared me down to my very toes. "And if The Magician is behind this in any way, we need to stop him. And quickly."

At that, she vanished with one of my French fries in her hand.

The stunned silence around the office matched how I felt.

I just wish I had a clue what was happening.

And how she seemed to know something that was going to happen in two days.

And who the hell The Magician was.

CHAPTER TWO

Everyone had stopped eating.

Terri was just shaking her head, her long black hair going back and forth around her face.

Madge was frowning, never a good sign when a waitress used to attempting to smile was frowning.

Stan looked angry and Patty looked confused, just as I was feeling.

"Time for milkshakes," Madge said.

At that moment every bit of food on the table vanished and Madge turned and stepped through the door back to the Diner.

The group had a habit of ordering milkshakes when we were working on a problem. Usually only big problems. So Madge thought this problem big enough for milkshakes and had cleared the table.

Again not a good sign.

I stared at the place on the booth where my French fries had been and kind of wished I had the power to bring them back. And then I wondered where they had gone, and then finally decided I didn't want to know any of those details. Not at the moment, anyway.

I glanced around at my team, then decided that none of them were going to speak, so it was up to me to be my normal clueless self and ask dumb questions. Sometimes my dumb questions got to the heart of the problem facing us, sometimes they just made me look silly for asking.

I wanted to start with how someone knew what was going to happen two days in the future, but decided on something more basic. "So someone want to give me the background on The Magician?"

"Right now he goes by Nick Scipio," Stan said without looking up. "He's been around for longer than anyone knows for certain. The protector and father, basically, of modern magic. Over the centuries he's taken many names when free, from Dedi in Egypt to Robert-Houdin."

"Is he a god?" Patty asked.

"He's an elf," Stan said.

I moaned. We had dealt a number of times with the elves and trolls and their fights. Because I had caught the one person causing elves and trolls to always battle, I was honored in their hidden casino here in Vegas, but I seldom went there. Just often enough to not insult them by never going there.

"You said something about him being free?" Screamer

asked, and Terri nodded beside him, her black hair moving around her face.

"He is sort of locked up in a time cell," Stan said, "between moments of time, that should make it impossible for him to escape. But he often does. It's been a good fifty years since his last escape, at least that I heard about."

"So why make all the 13th floors disappear?" I asked.

"You could ask him yourself," Madge said, appearing from the doorway of the Diner carrying six milkshakes.

Behind her strolled a tall, thin man with black hair covering the tips of his pointed ears. He wore a white frilly shirt like he was on the way to a wedding and a long, black cape. In one hand he carried a cane, but clearly didn't need it.

"I figured Madge would know where you all met," he said, his voice low and soothing in an odd way.

He looked around at the view, clearly impressed, then he stopped in front of the booth and bowed slightly. "The Magician at your service. And I want to be very clear that I will have nothing to do with the building floors disappearing in just under two days. But I must admit, it's a nice bit. I kind of wish I had thought of it."

He pulled up a chair and sat on it, facing all of us.

"Vanilla as always," Madge asked, placing the milkshake in front of him and then continuing on with the rest of ours.

"A wonderful memory," The Magician said. "Now a glass of fine whiskey and a cigar and I would be as happy as can be."

"Drink your milkshake, Nick," Madge said, shaking her

head and moving off to one side behind the booth. She never sat with us, but often took part in the meetings and it was clear she had no desire to miss this one.

"Good seeing you again, Stan," The Magician said, as he stirred his milkshake and sipped it.

I stared at Stan, then back at Nick Scipio, The Magician. Clearly they had history. And I was just about to ask what that history was when Lady Luck appeared and scooted into the booth beside her daughter.

"Nick," she said, nodding.

The Magician bowed slightly. "I am honored, as always."

"Cut the crap," Laverne said, "and explain to me what's happening and how you know about it."

When Lady Luck gets blunt, things really have to be going wrong. This just looked worse and worse by the moment.

Chapter Three

The Magician didn't let Lady Luck's brashness even seem to phase him. He took a sip of his milkshake, nodded a thank-you in Madge's direction, and then turned to face Lady Luck. From my position beside Patty across from Teri and her mother, I could see Nick's dark eyes. And I watched them closely as he spoke, seeing if I could get a read on him and if he was lying.

"In my little confines," The Magician said, "which are very comfortable, I might add, I have sometimes been able to see out ahead in time. Not far, and often not that accurately, since the future is always in flux by events of the present. But I did see that in two days all the 13th floors of every building in Las Vegas will become invisible. For some reason, all authorities will, at the time, know this will happen and will have all the floors from twelve-up completely evacuated. It will cause a very large event that will be difficult at best to explain away, except as a magician's illusion gone horribly wrong."

"I know all that," Laverne said, waving her hand in dismissal. "So who could actually pull off this kind of illusion?"

"Besides me?" The Magician asked. "No one. Which is why I don't think this is an illusion."

"Magic?" Stan asked as Lady Luck frowned.

Silence fell over the booth. And I had no idea why so many of them were upset. We were sitting in a booth in an invisible office five hundred feet above the MGM Grand Hotel and Casino. If that wasn't magic, what were we talking about?

"So who could pull off this level of magic?" Lady Luck finally asked. "And why would anyone break the ban?"

I wanted to scream WHAT BAN? But instead I just sat watching The Magician. From what I could tell, he had been telling the truth and seemed as worried as the rest of the people around the table.

I'm sure I looked worried as well, but not for the same reason. I was worried because I had no idea what they were talking about.

"I don't know the answer to that," The Magician said. "But I will be glad to help find out. If this actually happens, it will give all magicians a bad name and magicians in general will take the blame since it will be the only way to explain away such an event."

"Thanks," Lady Luck said, nodding. "You up for talking to your people?"

He took another long sip of the vanilla milkshake, then nodded. "Let's go."

"The rest of you keep working on this," Laverne said.

And she and The Magician vanished.

I sat there in the silence they left behind, so confused I didn't even have a question to ask. So Patty got the ball rolling.

"What did he do?"

Stan shook his head. "Not much, actually. Just pissed off the wrong god at the wrong time with a stupid trick. He and Laverne actually like each other, so she put him in a comfortable cell to keep him out of the way for a few centuries. He comes out, or as he likes to call it, "escapes" when he wants or needs to."

"So," I said, taking a deep breath, "someone want to explain to me the difference in magic and what is holding this office in the air?"

Screamer and Teri both laughed and Stan just shook his head. Patty just patted my leg, which meant my question was really stupid.

"Real magic," Teri said, "not the illusions that magicians do, is powered from the dark side. It does not come from any one person or skill, but by tapping into the pool of dark energy that rests just under the surface of everything."

Stan nodded and looked at me. "Your power to teleport, step between moments of time, and keep this place in the air comes from you, the depth of your ability to help others. It is a power of your mind and who you are. Just as studying another person and knowing how they are going to act in a hand of cards is a trained skill.

"Okay," was all I could manage to say. I sure didn't feel like I had a powerful mind. Far from it at the moment, in fact.

"That's why some of us can see slightly into the future as well," Stan said. "Like you watch a person and can predict a play or know his cards, others can watch life and know what might be possible in the future. A skill."

Well, that sort of explained that question at least, so I nodded.

He looked squarely at me and then went on, his tone and voice very, very clear. "All our powers are powers of light and come out of who we are and our own skills and talents. Nothing we do is actually magic."

I decided to just keep pushing my ignorance out there for everyone to see. "So this stunt of making entire floors invisible comes from a magic that is banned?"

Stan and Terri both nodded.

Stan said, "Actual magic has been banned for centuries, but some people try it anyway at times."

"And what happens to them?" Patty asked.

"The dark magic consumes them," Screamer said, his voice sounding disgusted. "And they became part of the dark pool of power. Not something I would ever want to experience. Think of the worst images of hell and multiply that by one hundred."

With that the silence just settled over the room again. Outside the windows, the sun was shining, planes were landing at the airport, and the world kept going, unaware that entire slices of buildings were about to vanish.

I took a sip of my milkshake and let the coolness calm me a little. I just couldn't get one word out of my head and I finally just blurted it out. "Why?"

"Why do they get consumed?" Screamer asked, looking at me as if I had lost my mind completely.

"No," I said, shaking my head. "Why make floors invisible? If this really is someone using magic and risking his or her life to do so, why do this stunt? It seems very petty, has no obvious return for the stunt, and flat makes no sense."

And yet again the silence filled my office around the booth.

I was right.

I knew it. And their lack of an answer confirmed that for me.

No one who knew how to do dark magic and the repercussions from the use of dark magic would ever do something this stupid and out in the open.

And for no gain that I could see.

Suddenly I had yet another idea.

"What happens if this isn't real dark magic? What happens if it is a superhero having some issues with power control?"

Stan looked at me with a look that I couldn't read, but

that wasn't unusual for me with Stan. He was the God of Poker, after all.

"Are you suggesting," Screamer asked, leaning forward, "that what is about to happen to all the 13th floors might be nothing more than an accident about to happen?"

"Possible," I said. "So what kind of superhero needs to learn to make things vanish in their training?"

Teri started to say something, then shut her mouth and shook her head.

Screamer just shook his head.

Stan and Patty both said nothing.

Finally, from behind the booth Madge said, "Cleaners. And some food superheroes as well."

"Like you made our lunch remains vanish," I said, glancing back at her.

She nodded.

"Are there Gods of Cleaners and Superheroes of cleaning?" I asked, then knew the answer. Of course there were. I had watched a person come into a room and it seemed to just get clean, as if by some sort of magic, which was more-than-likely a special power. I always admired people who could do that type of cleaning, since every time I tried to clean something, it looked worse instead of better.

"Damn," Stan said softly. Then he said, "Everyone's with me."

"Except me," Madge said. "I'll have milkshakes ready for you when you get back."

Stan nodded and then a moment later all five of us were standing in a huge warehouse that smelled of ammonia and other cleaning solutions.

CHAPTER FOUR

The building around us was so large I couldn't see any wall in any direction. Nothing but aisles between huge stacks of cases of what looked like varied cleaning solutions and supplies.

The roof had to be ten stories overhead, the lights dim, the floor smooth concrete, and the temperature worse than air conditioning set too low. The stack closest to me had to go up four or five stories into the air, pallet on top of pallet. How they stayed stacked like that was anyone's guess, or how anyone did the stacking was another skill I really didn't want to watch anytime soon.

A moment after we arrived, the Magician and Lady Luck arrived as well.

She turned to me. "You think this might be a new super-hero having issues with powers?"

I nodded. "An idea that makes sense. Other than to do as an illusion, this future event makes no sense otherwise."

The Magician nodded. "Now I see why these people hang around with you."

"Thanks," I said, "but why are we standing here in this warehouse?"

"What, you don't like my office or something?" a voice blurted behind me.

I spun around to face a short, stout, matronly woman wearing a light blue cleaning uniform. On the cloth sewn-on name badge it read "Hygieia" and under that it said in small letters "Call me Jean."

Laverne stepped up in front of me to face the new woman before I could say anything about her "office."

"Jean, thanks for meeting with us," Laverne said, her voice very stern, so much so that I shuddered slightly. "Every 13th floor of every building in Las Vegas is going to vanish in just under two days."

"Good," Jean said, shrugging. "We won't have to clean them."

"We think it's one of your people who is going to cause the problem," Laverne said.

She frowned at Laverne, started to say something, then stopped and really looked around at all of us. "Stan, Poker Boy, Patty Ledgerwood, Screamer, your daughter, and The Magician. You have the A-Team on this, so it must be serious."

"It is," Laverne said. "Very serious. We can't let this happen. Are you training someone in the Las Vegas area?"

"Always training someone it seems," Jean said.

Beside her a very, very short man appeared wearing a hood over his head and only allowing just part of his face to show. I had no idea who he was or what his job was.

"You are training one called Dee, my sister," the short man said, his voice very deep.

"Oh, yeah, her," Jean said, nodding. "She's a strange talent, very powerful, only been on the job a few months, but seems to learn quickly."

"She has many fears," the short man said. Then he vanished.

At that point I had about fifty questions I wanted to ask, but as I had learned years before, when dealing with Gods, it was better to just keep silent and let them go on and then have someone explain later what happened.

"I'm not sure how Dee having fears could cause this," Jean said, looking puzzled.

"Maybe she's afraid of the number thirteen," I said, instantly breaking my rule about keeping my mouth shut.

Silence.

And in a huge warehouse with the ceiling towering four stories over my head, that silence seemed awful loud as everyone stared at me.

Finally Jean said, "I will bring Dee."

I instantly felt sorry for the poor girl. If I had been

brought into a group like this, I would have more than likely fainted during my first years of being a superhero.

"Hold on," I said before the God of Cleaning could jump away. "I'm afraid, as a new superhero, she won't be able to answer any questions with a crowd like this. This group still intimidates me at times and I've been at this for a decade or so."

Jean nodded. "What would you suggest, Poker Boy?"

"Patty and I could go talk with her alone and the rest of you can keep track of how the conversation goes."

Jean glanced at Laverne who nodded.

"She is working on the third floor of the Golden Nugget. Tall, skinny, very young and very smart."

"Blind camera spot end of the hall," Stan said, "against the wall across from the elevators."

I nodded and jumped with Patty to that spot.

Chapter Five

Faint music played in the hallway and it smelled like the carpets had just been vacuumed. Down the plush hallway to our right was a maid's cart, so we headed in that direction.

As we neared the cart a tall woman with red hair appeared wearing a maid's uniform and carrying an armload of towels. She smiled at us, then dropped the towels into her cart. She was very young and hadn't yet seemed to grow into her body or her face.

It was clearly Dee. Under the sleeves of her shirt I could see signs of tattoos and another tattoo peaked out of her high collar.

As she started to turn back to go into the room I said, "Dee, we need to talk with you."

She stopped, suddenly looking puzzled. Her bright green eyes got very round.

"I am Poker Boy, this is Patty Ledgerwood."

Patty extended her hand. "Great to meet you," Patty said, giving the young superhero her best calming power.

Dee shook Patty's hand and seemed to relax a little. I didn't add in my calming power just yet, but I had a hunch I was going to need it.

"Your boss, Jean, says great things about you," I said.

Suddenly Dee looked panicked again. I remember early on in my superhero starting months, I thought no one knew I was secretly a superhero, so I was always shocked when another person knew that. Like me, she was going to be surprised as she learned just how many superheroes and gods there really were.

At the end of the hallway, the elevator dinged and the door started to open. So I slipped us out of time and into an instant between moments of time so that we wouldn't be disturbed. Since we were in a hallway and couldn't hear any traffic noise outside, nothing seemed to change, so Dee didn't notice.

"How do you know Jean?" Dee asked, looking first at Patty, who was still smiling and then back at me.

"We know many of the different gods," Patty said. "I work in the hospitality area and Poker Boy here works in the poker area, just as you work in the cleaning area. We are all at the same level, just under different departments."

Dee nodded and relaxed again. This girl really, really was the nervous type, of that there was no doubt.

I decided since Jean and Laverne and Stan were watching, to just jump to the problem. "Dee, are you scheduled in two days to clean Floor 14 here?"

Panic flipped across Dee's face and I sent calming waves at her, just as Patty was doing, trying to help her stay under control. I could feel my calming and trust-me power boosted a little as well, more than likely from Stan.

Dee calmed down and then nodded. "It's the 13th floor and I'm deathly afraid of it. I don't know what to do."

"We can help," Patty said, smiling as both of us kept aiming our combined calming powers at the young superhero. We were hitting Dee with so much calming juice, we could have put a horse to sleep smiling.

"But it's part of my job to clean that floor," Dee said, looking like she was about to burst into tears.

Suddenly I had another idea.

"We can help with that if you let us," I said. "We can help you never fear anything with the number 13 again."

"You could do that?" Dee asked. "And Jean wouldn't mind?"

"If it's going to help you do your job," Patty said, "I'm sure she wouldn't mind at all."

Dee stared at me, then at Patty for a moment. I could feel Stan boosting my "trust me" power I was pouring at Dee.

Finally Dee nodded.

"Stan, bring Screamer," I said into the air.

A moment later Stan and Screamer appeared.

Dee jumped. "Are you gods?"

"He is," Screamer said, smiling at Dee as he pointed at Stan. "Great to meet you, Dee."

Screamer extended his hand and the moment he touched Dee, she froze.

Patty and I kept our calming powers aimed at Dee and turned up to full power.

"Need help to clean this out, Stan," Screamer said.

Stan nodded and touched Screamer's shoulder. I knew at that moment in time they were both inside Dee's mind, working to clear out her fears of the number thirteen without really hurting her or changing her in any way and leaving no trace they had been in there.

After a moment Stan nodded and dropped his hand from Screamer's shoulder. Then Screamer let go of Dee's hand.

"So what can you do to help me?" Dee asked, staring at Screamer and then at Stan.

"Do you still fear the number thirteen?" I asked.

She frowned for a moment, then shook her head. "No, I don't. Wow, you guys are good."

"We'll let you get back to work now," Patty said, touching Dee's arm one more time to really leave a calming and pleasant feel with the young superhero.

"Thanks," Dee said, smiling. "I hope to see you again."

As I dropped the time shield and jumped all of us back to my office in the air over the MGM Grand Hotel, all I kept thinking about was that I had no doubt we were going to see more of that young superhero in the future. I had a hunch she might just be helping the team down the road at times.

I guess that was my way of seeing into the future a little.

Madge was waiting for us with freshly made milkshakes. Laverne and The Magician and Terri appeared a moment after we did.

"Jean thanks you all," Laverne said. "As do I."

"I thank you as well," The Magician said, bowing slightly. "Your quick thinking and action has saved illusionists everywhere from a very difficult black eye."

Smiling, I slid into the booth and Patty slid in beside me as Terri gave Screamer a big kiss and then joined us.

It had seemed like hours ago that my French fries had disappeared from the table, but actually, this time, we had saved the city in just under a half hour.

"Madge," I asked, smiling at her as she placed the last milkshake on the table, "is there any chance you could make those French fries reappear?"

"Make that two orders," Lady Luck said, sliding into the booth beside her daughter.

"Three, if you don't mind," The Magician said, pulling up a chair.

Madge laughed and turned for the door to the Diner. "I had a hunch you would want some after lunch got shortened, so four orders of fries are cooking right now."

"Seeing the future again, Miss Madge?" The Magician asked, winking.

She smiled at him and winked back. "Depends if you have enough magic up that sleeve of yours to handle a future me."

"Have I ever failed you, Miss Madge?"

Madge laughed like a young girl and disappeared through the door.

All Patty and I and Screamer and Terri could do was just stare open-mouthed at The Magician as he sipped on his milkshake, smiling.

Lady Luck just shook her head as I tried desperately to clear the image out of my mind of a tall, skinny elf and an overweight waitress together.

I have a hunch it's burned there forever.

Just Shoot Me Now!

Chapter One

The little jerk cherub just kept fluttering around near the ceiling of the poker room at Spirit Winds Casino. He acted like a bird trapped inside a small room with no windows. I know he was trying to get my attention, but the last thing I wanted to deal with tonight was a cherub.

And actually he had a couple small birds with very long beaks with him and they seemed to be flying in a figure-eight pattern, just missing each other as they moved around and around over my head.

The game was as good as a five-ten no limit gets. Three tourists who were drinking and wanting to have the action, two weak regulars, and two professionals. Plus me.

I had died and gone to heaven, cherub and all, it seemed. I was already three hundred up and the night was still young.

Nothing can get my blood going more than a high-action poker game with players I know I can beat.

But nothing can put a player off his game more than a circling cherub.

I glanced up at the cherub and his two bird friends as I tossed a seven-four off-suit into the muck. No one else in the room could see the little idiot fluttering around the lights. He had golden hair and wore a white cloth wrapped around him that looked more like a diaper in places than anything else. The cloth started at one ankle and ended up over his shoulder.

His white wings were fluttering constantly like a humming bird's and he had on the traditional fake cherub halo that seemed to glow bright yellow. They could take those halo things off like a hat. He was about three feet tall at most and wore no shoes.

I even knew this one's name. Chadwick.

Chadwick the Cherub.

I had dealt with him once before on an assignment to help out a woman who thought she was dying and had started to give away her vast fortune. It turned out old Chadwick was just showing himself to her like a bad flasher, making her think she was seeing an angel with a very small penis.

He was sent to cherub counseling after I stopped him from forcing the poor woman to end up broke and insane and permanently put off of sex.

Now it seemed he was back. And was just as annoying. At least this time he was keeping his cloth diaper where it belonged.

I tried to ignore him again for another hand, but ignoring a kid-sized mythical creature fluttering over your head is hard to do.

Finally I couldn't handle it anymore. I flipped into the muck a couple suited connectors and froze time.

Actually I didn't really freeze time. No one could do that. But I did have the power to step between moments in time. It felt like I had frozen time because all the sounds of the casino stopped, and everyone froze in that moment.

Everyone but me and Chadwick.

His two bird friends remained frozen as well up near the ceiling. And some bird poop was stopped in midair headed for a spot right in front of my chips. Great, just great.

I stood and looked up at the cherub who had stopped flying around and was just hovering, looking down at me with a smile.

"All right, let's get to this," I said.

He came down and hovered in front of me, his white wings moving so fast that they looked like they were standing still. His smile was a cross between a worried grin and a smirk showing how happy he was I had come around.

"Nice trick on this time thing," he said, indicating the frozen people around us. "I thought only gods could do this."

"Just park it and take off that stupid halo," I said.

He stopped and stood on the nearest empty poker table. He folded his wings back behind him and stuffed the halo into his white cloth diaper strip where it wrapped up and over his shoulder like a sling.

"First off," I said, not even trying to hide how annoyed I was, "does Cherry know you are here?"

Cherry was the head cherub and one of the nicer creatures I had ever had the pleasure to meet.

Chadwick nodded. "She's the one who sent me."

His voice was deep and rough, not at all like what his image would project. He sounded more like a cigar-smoking old man. Most cherubs were thousands of years old. My boss, Stan the God of Poker had told me that Cherry was far older than he was which meant she was thousands and thousands of years old at least.

More than likely Chadwick was a few thousand years old as well.

"And I can check that?" I asked, calling Chadwick's bluff.

"Yes," he said.

He wasn't lying. I could tell a lie on a cherub's face from across the room. It seemed the sweet look didn't give them much chance to lie, especially to poker players. Cherry actually had suggested he come talk to me.

Great. Just great. A perfect night just ruined. Could someone just shoot me now?

Chapter Two

"So what do you need from me?" I asked, almost afraid of the question's answer.

Good old Chadwick looked me direct in the eyes with those round, innocent-looking brown eyes of his and said, "I want to be part of your team."

I actually managed to not break out into complete gales of laughter.

The team he was talking about consisted of three other superheroes and one god that helped me solve major cases. We often saved the world.

Me and my girlfriend and sidekick, Patty Ledgerwood, aka Front Desk Girl, led the team. Patty was a superhero working in the hospitality side of the world.

The third member was Screamer, a man able to read

minds and connect minds at times. Screamer was a superhero who worked in the law enforcement branch of the gods.

The fourth member was The Smoke, a part dog, part human who was a superhero working for the gods of animals.

And then there was Stan, the God of Poker, my boss. He was our connection to Laverne, Lady Luck herself.

And now Chadwick the Flasher Cherub wanted to join the team.

Somehow I kept most of my poker face locked on and smiled and asked him the next question.

"Why would you want to do that?"

"Oh, I personally don't," Chadwick said. "But Cherry thinks it would be a good idea for me to start doing something constructive with my time now that I am mostly done with my counseling sessions."

I sort of stared at the chubby little cherub for a moment, trying to understand what I had just heard.

I must be dreaming. I had to be. I was at such a perfect table, a perfect poker game, the kind of game that just didn't happen every night. And now I was dealing with a converted flasher who wanted to join my team, but who really didn't want to join my team.

And a bird was about to poop on my poker table.

This had to be a nightmare, a really bad one.

I had no idea what to do.

I wanted to just laugh and send him back to Cherry, but my little voice was telling me that wouldn't be a good idea. There had to be some politics involved with all this and for a superhero to get involved with politics among the different gods was never a good idea.

I looked at Chadwick again.

"What can it hurt?" he asked, shrugging.

I couldn't begin to answer that, since most of the time that the team worked together on a problem, the entire world was at stake.

I looked up at the ceiling and shouted, "Stan!"

I needed help and I needed it fast. Before I said something I would regret and maybe cause a rift between different branches of gods, as if there weren't enough of those already.

Stan appeared beside me, inside the frozen time instant I had created. Stan wore his normal gray sweater, dark slacks, and blank expression. He was slightly shorter than I was and looked like any person you might see on the street. As the God of Poker, he could blend in anywhere and it was impossible to read any emotion on his face unless he wanted you to, or didn't care.

"Hi, Stan," Chadwick said, waving a chubby little hand at the God of Poker.

"I was afraid of this," Stan said.

"That's not making me feel any better," I said. "Chadwick here wants to join my team."

"Yeah, I heard," Stan said.

"But he really doesn't," I said. "Do you, Chadwick?"

"Oh, hell no," the cherub said. "It sounds like far too much work. It was just Cherry's idea."

"You know what I told you about swearing," a woman's voice said from above us.

I looked up as Cherry fluttered to a stop on the table next to a suddenly worried Chadwick.

She looked almost identical to Chadwick, except her golden hair was longer and the diaper-like cloth also covered her chest. Her face was thinner as well and she had a beauty to her that took my breath away.

"Sorry," Chadwick said, looking down.

"Nice seeing you again, Cherry," Stan said.

"I agree," I said, bowing slightly to her. "You look more radiant than ever."

She smiled and I could feel the warmth filling the air around me. "There's a real reason a lot of the gods like you, Poker Boy," she said.

"He's a charmer all right," Stan said, shaking his head. "So tell me why you think it would be a good idea for Chadwick here to join Poker Boy's team?"

"Keep Chadwick focused and out of trouble," Cherry said. "He needs something to hold his attention."

"Besides human women," Stan said before I could. Thankfully.

"Yes," Cherry said. "To be honest."

I knew now how to solve the problem. I just had to find good old Chadwick something to do. I had no idea what, but anything was better than him hanging around my team.

"You know we seldom put the team together," I said to

Cherry. "In fact, it has been almost two months since the entire team has needed to be together for a problem."

"Oh," Cherry said, the smile vanishing from her face. "That's not going to work. I thought you met and worked every day together."

"Not even every month," Stan said, backing up my play.

Chadwick actually looked relieved. Cherry looked completely devastated for some reason.

I needed to come up with an idea and come up with it quick.

I sort of turned to Chadwick. "Besides human women, what do you like?"

"I don't even like them that much," Chadwick said.

Cherry turned slightly away and rolled her eyes, which made Stan grin.

Then Cherry said, "His mother married a Putti, so there is a lot of the old Cupid blood in him."

"So, Chadwick," I said. "What exactly are your powers that would help my team?"

I figured that if I could learn what he could do, I might be able to come up with a way to get him busy with something else. Anything else.

Chadwick looked annoyed, but Cherry looked at him and he took a deep breath and turned to face me directly.

"I can fly. I can be invisible. I can pass through any wall. I am an expert spy and can remember everything to the word anyone says that I am listening to and report that back exactly. Because of my father, I am an expert with the magical bow and arrow, but am not allowed to carry one because of an incident a number of decades back with a movie star and a president."

With that he glared at Cherry who only shrugged. "You tried to interfere with human events. You will serve your sentence to the fullest."

Chadwick just shook his head and looked down.

"How fast can you fly?" I asked.

"I can be in Las Vegas faster than you can jump there with your teleporting superpower."

Both Stan and Cherry nodded at that.

I was surprised. Now that I was actually thinking about it, there was no doubt Chadwick would be a good addition to the team on some problems. None of us had the abilities he had.

I glanced at Stan who actually looked like he was thinking the same thing.

"Chadwick," I said, "honestly I think we can use you at times on our team. We don't use every member every mission, but I think your powers would add to our team on certain missions."

Stan was nodding.

Cherry was looking surprised, and Chadwick looked shocked.

"You're kidding, right?" Chadwick asked.

"Not in the slightest," I said. "But the problem is we don't often have missions and you need something to keep you occupied."

"To help you keep that thing in your diapers," Stan said.

"It's not a diaper," Chadwick said in his gruff voice, glaring at Stan.

"Poker Boy is right," Cherry said, nodding to me with thanks. "If you want to be on Poker Boy's team, which is a very high honor, you need to stay out of trouble and do something constructive."

"And just what would that be?" Chadwick asked, looking disgusted. "I've been bored for most of the last thousand years. Being a cherub just doesn't have a lot of purpose these days. So I'm open to suggestions."

Because we were between a moment in time, the frozen poker room around us was deadly silent and now the four of us were as well. I just couldn't think of a thing for Chadwick to do.

Nothing.

Chapter Three

I glanced up and saw the two frozen birds that he had brought in with him. And the bird poop hanging in midair like a promise yet to be kept.

"What's with the birds?" I asked, trying to buy some time to think.

"I like birds and they like me," he said. "It's fun flying with them."

I had a faint glimmering of an idea, but I wasn't sure about it. I needed more information.

"Can you talk to them?"

"Not much," Chadwick said. "They aren't that smart."

I turned to Stan and Cherry. "Is there a god of birds? Or a god who looks over that area of the animal kingdom?"

Both Stan and Cherry looked puzzled.

"Not really," Stan said. "The Smoke's boss would be the

most likely, but most gods tend to have one bird or another that they favor, but no one that I know is over all the birds in general."

"So they have no god really looking out for them?" I asked, surprised. I thought every aspect of the world had a god over it.

"I wouldn't think so," Cherry said looking very puzzled. "Odd, don't you think?"

I turned to Chadwick. "How about you make it your job to save birds and watch out over them?"

He just looked puzzled.

"You said you like them, right?" I asked.

He nodded.

"And you can fly faster than any bird, right?"

"Yeah," he said.

"So make it your job to save birds. If a bird is about to fly in front of a truck, save it. Save birds trapped in a cage in a burning house. Save birds from being shot by kids."

Both Cherry and Stan were smiling, so I knew I had them on board with the idea.

And Chadwick was nodding slowly as he thought about it.

"There is clearly no one else doing it," I said. "And from the number of dead birds I've seen over the years, clearly it needs to be done."

Chadwick nodded. "I've saved a few birds along the way and it always felt good."

"Cherry," I said, turning to Chadwick's boss, "you want

to check with the appropriate god in charge to make sure it would be all right if Chadwick took up this great mission?"

"I think it will be," she said, smiling at me and looking very relieved.

I turned back to Chadwick. "And I'll still need you on my team on some missions if that's all right with you. Your special powers could really help at times."

Chadwick was nodding and smiling. "Sure, sure, and if I find something big that I need help on, I can get your help as well?"

"Of course," I said, smiling. "The entire team if need be."

"Great," he said.

He turned to Cherry. "I really like this idea. Much better than going around shooting people with stupid magic arrows like my dad does."

"I agree," Cherry said. "It is a perfect mission for you. Perfect, and will do a ton of good."

"Thanks, Poker Boy," Chadwick said.

"Yes, thank you," Cherry said.

And then they were both gone along with the two birds, but the big drop of bird poop still hung there.

"Looks like you have a new member of the team," Stan said, shaking his head. "Hard to imagine."

I just laughed. "Patty is never going to believe that I invited Chadwick the Famous Flashing Cherub to join the team."

"If he can keep the little thing in his diaper," Stan said, also laughing, "he just might be able to help at times."

"He might at that," I said. "But if nothing else we saved a lot of birds tonight."

Stan vanished, but I could still hear him laughing.

I grabbed a couple handfuls of napkins and went back to my chair at the poker table. I placed the napkin under the bird poop and then let myself slip back into the time stream.

The noise of the casino crashed in around me as the bird poop hit the napkins and I swept them up before anyone noticed.

I just hoped that cleaning up crap wasn't a sign of the times ahead with Chadwick the Flashing Cherub.

Leaking Away A Life

CHAPTER ONE

I was in a really nice no-limit game at my home casino, the Spirit Winds Casino in the Oregon Coastal Mountain Range. The night was still young, five tourists were playing fast with a lot of extra money, and there was only one other pro on the table besides me and we were staying out of each other's way just fine.

I had found heaven in a poker game.

And heaven was paying off nicely so far. After two hours I was five hundred up and considering how much the tourists were drinking, I hoped that number would get much, much higher before I had to leave.

My girlfriend, Patty Ledgerwood, aka Front Desk Girl, and I were building a new home on property I owned up in the mountains near the casino. I had teleported, or jumped as I liked to call it, from Vegas up here to check on the house and then had decided to just stay and play since Patty didn't get off work until one in the morning from the MGM Grand Hotel front desk.

I had more money than I sometimes knew what to do with, since I won a lot and spent almost nothing. We had decided to build a custom home with every modern feature and everything we wanted. Patty had loved designing it.

I had saved the life of one of the best contractors in the world, a guy by the name of Bob Davis, by offering him a job building the house. So far the construction had taken just over two years, but it was almost done.

And spectacular didn't begin to describe the home. Way beyond my class as a human being, that's for sure, with all the glass, mahogany and stone, and the beautiful kitchen, to say nothing of the four modern bathrooms.

Patty absolutely loved the place, and she and Bob got along like old friends.

When Bob and his crew were done here, Patty and I were going to keep him on salary with a huge raise and have him build Patty and me a home in Las Vegas as well. Since we could teleport anywhere we wanted instantly, I wasn't sure we needed two homes. But Patty liked the idea and I sure had enough money to afford the two homes and a couple hundred more like it.

Playing poker had been really good to me, of that there was no doubt. And besides these two homes, I spent almost nothing except to buy some food at times and pay my taxes.

I was just about to raise one of the tourists at the table a smooth hundred bucks when my boss, Stan, the God of Poker, froze time around me and appeared next to the table.

Stan was dressed in his usual sweater vest, tan slacks, and polished shoes. His short brown hair and plain face make him the most unmemorable person you could ever meet. He liked it that way.

Me, on the other hand, I wanted to be remembered. I always wore what I called my uniform. A black leather coat and a black fedora-like hat. When I had first started playing, I sometimes also wore black mirror sunglasses but had given those up fairly quickly as having no value. The only person on the planet who had a better poker face than I did was Stan.

Sometimes I wanted people to think they had a read on me. I made a lot of money from those idiots.

I stood and moved over to Stan. He actually hadn't stopped time, just taken us in-between moments in time. But if felt like time had stopped since everyone was frozen and all sounds of the casino had vanished.

"We got a problem?" I asked.

He usually only came and got me like this when the team had a major problem to solve, like saving the entire planet or something.

"No team problem," Stan said. "But I need your help on something."

Now that stunned me more than I wanted to say. Stan never asked for my help personally. He was a god. I was a superhero who worked for him. What could I actually do to help him?

"The Kid needs some help," he said.

The Kid was the other poker superhero working for Stan. Usually I would have been enough, but since I spent so much time on larger problems with our team, Stan had gotten a second superhero.

I liked The Kid, as he called himself. He was about twenty-six now, had a great heart and a love of the game. He was good, very good.

"So what's he dealing with?" I asked, figuring The Kid had gotten himself into trying to solve a problem beyond his experience.

"He has a leak," Stan said.

Now at that I just blinked. I knew exactly what he meant by "a leak." Professional poker players who play other games such as sports books or blackjack or worse yet, slot machines, are said to have a "leak." They win their money at poker and leak all their winnings out through losses in areas they can't control like they control a poker game.

They do it for the thrill, some say. I could never see the point, actually.

It had never, ever occurred to me to play any of the other games in a casino mainly because I knew the odds. That is just recreation for people and fine for people to come and enjoy the time.

Poker, on the other hand, is a game of skill and is often called a sport by many.

As in any sport, there is some luck, but skill always wins out in poker in the long run.

In other games in casinos, the casinos always win out in the long run. Always. That's the design of the games and how they build the big buildings with all the flashing lights.

"How bad is it?" I asked Stan.

"Bad," Stan said. "He's living in his car, can't play any game but grinds in 3-6 limit because he has no bankroll to buy in to larger games."

"Skill doesn't help him much in those games," I said.

Then I just shook my head. I had enough money in a dozen banks to buy half a city. That's because I was good at poker, seldom spent anything I won, and had no leaks.

"He can't be helping what you need him for in that condition."

Stan nodded. "He's not at all, and he's hitting bottom now, which is why I came for you. I'm afraid we might lose him."

I nodded. I had heard it happened. Superheroes sometimes, in their early years, just couldn't handle the job and often lost all their powers or just killed themselves. I would hate to see that happen to anyone.

But I wasn't sure exactly what to do. A professional poker player with a leak was called a problem gambler. And that took real professional help to fix.

"Got any ideas what we can do?" I asked Stan.

He just shook his head and even on his poker face I could read sadness. He liked The Kid, I could tell.

We stood there in the intense silence of the frozen casino for a moment, then I had a slight idea.

A problem gambler needed real help. Someone needed to get The Kid to understand that the other games in a casino were bad news while letting him keep his powers at the poker table.

This was not going to be easy in any stretch of the imagination.

More than likely impossible.

But they had to try.

Chapter Two

"Who is the God in the area of counseling?" I asked Stan.

"Overall in charge is Victor, but out of the question to contact him," Stan said. "He's one of the long-term major gods who is seldom seen over the centuries.

"Lower gods?" I asked. "Someone who might help on something like this?"

Stan looked doubtful, so I changed up the question. "How about a young superhero in that area?" I asked. "A young woman, good-looking and smart, new as a superhero, and up for a massive challenge with The Kid."

Stan saw where I was headed and nodded. "Cash out and I'll go find out and be back."

I went back to my seat and Stan released the time bubble.

The sounds of the casino smashed into me like a hard wave. I would never get used to that. Ever.

I finished the hand, took another few hundred of the tourist's money, then pretended to glance at my phone. "Wife wants me home," I said.

A lie that everyone at the table understood just fine.

I racked up my chips as everyone said goodbye to a lot of their money, all in good spirits. A minute later I had the seven hundred I had won for the night in my pocket and was headed for the poker room door into the casino when Stan again froze time around me.

And again everyone stopped and all sound went away.

Stan had a young woman with him. She had on a light knit sweater and a blue blouse under it, with jeans and tennis shoes. She looked like she might be right out of college.

I was fairly certain I recognized her, but couldn't place from where.

Stan quickly introduced us. Her name was Gretchen and she had a wonderful smile and large, trusting brown eyes. I liked her at once, which I had a hunch was part of her powers.

From the way she was looking, she still wasn't used to teleporting anywhere.

Then Stan dropped a bombshell. "Gretchen is one of my daughters."

I opened my mouth and then closed it. Three years ago we had rescued Stan's two daughters from a time bubble that had trapped them since the days of Atlantis. That's where I recognized her from.

Clearly Gretchen had adapted well to this world and was moving on with her life.

"From Atlantis?" I asked.

"Born and raised there," she said, smiling. "Bet I don't look a day over twenty -three, huh?"

I laughed. "Not a day."

Stan hugged her.

Then he said, "I got permission from her boss to let her work at this problem for as long as it takes."

"Are you familiar with gambling addictions and problem gamblers?" I asked after she looked around, wide-eyed at the frozen people in the poker room and the casino beyond.

"Some," she said. "I have dealt with a few cases and of course, studied the problem through school, both here and back in college in Atlantis."

"Well, we have a real mess we hope you can help us with," I said. "Stan, you want to meet in my office?"

He nodded and they vanished.

And once again the sound of the casino smashed back in around me, making me shake my head. I loved casinos, everything about them. They gave me power and energy. But until all the sound in one was taken away, you never noticed how really loud they were.

I went out through the casino front door to a dead camera area in the parking lot and jumped from the mountains of Oregon to my invisible office that floated a thousand feet in the air over Las Vegas Boulevard.

Stan was sitting in the only real furniture in my office, a

huge horseshoe-shaped diner booth with red-vinyl seats and a scarred-up wood tabletop.

Gretchen was standing, holding onto the wood railing that went all the way around the glass walls of my office, staring at the view of the city a thousand feet below.

It really was an amazing view.

"I got Madge bringing us some fries and three milkshakes," Stan said.

"Wonderful," I said.

Madge was a superhero in the food services area and owned the diner where my team used to meet. After we built the office that I patterned after her booth, only larger, I put a portal from here to the diner so my team members who didn't teleport could come through, and Madge could treat this booth like another booth in her restaurant.

"I had heard about this office," Gretchen said, turning to look at us, her brown eyes even rounder than normal. "Never thought I would actually get to see it."

"Well," I said, indicating she should come and sit in the large booth. "That shows how much we really need your help on something very important to us."

"Dad said it was important as well, so why me?" she asked, turning and moving toward the booth.

"Because you are young, smart, new as a superhero, and an attractive woman," I said, being honest with her.

"And our problem person is young," Stan said, "new as a superhero, and an attractive man. And besides, your boss and I both think you would be perfect to try to help us."

At that, Gretchen just blushed as Stan stood to let Gretchen into the booth.

"Thank you, Daddy."

Hearing Stan called "Daddy" sort of took my breath away, but I managed to keep my stupid mouth shut.

Stan and I couldn't help The Kid. We were basically like parents to him and a parent sure couldn't tell a kid to not smoke or drink and have it stick. The Kid had a problem that needed to be solved not just for a year or so, but for centuries.

I had no idea if any of this was going to work. But as far as I was concerned, Gretchen was the only hope The Kid had of surviving.

We now had to explain why.

<h1 style="text-align:center">Chapter Three</h1>

After about ten minutes of Stan and me trying to give Gretchen a primer on professional poker players, I realized we were going to need help.

As Madge came in with the milkshakes and fries, I said, "Be right back. Going to see if Patty can take a break."

Stan nodded and actually looked a little relieved. It had become clear that we were not communicating with Gretchen in a language she seemed to understand. She was clearly brilliant, but all the terms were just off to her.

I jumped to the front of the MGM Grand Hotel front desk and froze time for everyone but me and Patty. "Got a situation we need a little help on."

"Team situation?" she asked, looking worried.

"Well, not really, but a team is forming to help the problem," I said. I quickly summarized what we were dealing with and why I thought it would be a good idea for her to help Stan's daughter, Gretchen, get a sense of what The Kid was facing as a professional poker player with a leak.

When I told her The Kid had a leak, she just looked sad and shook her head.

"You don't give him much chance, do you?" I asked.

She shook her head no. "Glad to help do what we can do. I'll talk to my boss and be there in five minutes."

I nodded and jumped back to my office, releasing the time bubble formed around us.

For the next five minutes, Stan and I and Gretchen talked about other things, such as building this office and some of the other team members who had helped save the world a few times. When Laverne's name came up, I thought Gretchen was going to faint dead away.

I remembered that feeling myself early on. Just the mention of Lady Luck's name often had me shaking.

Patty arrived looking great. She had changed out of her uniform into a tan blouse, jeans, and tennis shoes and she had her wonderful brown hair combed out. She was the most beautiful woman in the world as far as I was concerned.

"Told my boss a snippet of the problem and she let me take the rest of the night off to help," Patty said.

I stood and Patty scooted into the booth beside Gretchen. Instantly the two of them hit it off. Patty was good. She was really that good and one of her superpowers was that others just liked her. She had promised she had never used that on me. She said she hadn't needed to, since I fell head-over-heels for her the first time I met her.

Literally.

I tripped over some ropes in front of the desk she was working at.

She thought it cute. I had thought it mortally embarrassing.

With Patty's help, we slowly got Gretchen to understand The Kid's job as a professional poker player and how poker was not gambling.

"The Kid is a mathematician, a professional liar, a professional actor, and has a memory for cards next to none," I said. "He has the ability to read a person and almost know what they are thinking at a poker table, and those are his normal poker skills, not his superhero skills."

Gretchen was nodding. "So poker is a sport. I think I am starting to understand that."

"It is," Stan said. "A skill that takes years to learn and many do not learn it as well as The Kid has."

"Is he any good as a superhero?" Gretchen asked.

"He was before he ran into this gambling problem," Stan said. "He saved a bunch of lives, helped countless people and seemed to be enjoying what he was doing until the money issues overwhelmed him from his leak. Now he pays little attention to the superhero side of things."

"That's because he can't even help himself," I said, "so he feels I'm sure that he can't help others."

Everyone around the booth nodded.

"So what exactly is his leak, as you call it?" Gretchen said. "His addiction?"

"Sports book," Stan said.

I sighed and Patty just shook her head.

"Why is that bad?" Gretchen asked. "To be honest, I don't even know what a sports book is."

"Someone can place a wager on the outcome of some sporting event in a sports book in a casino," Stan said. "From horse racing to soccer games, you name it, it is bet on."

"It is a common leak for professional poker players," I said. "Because when you are sitting in a poker room, there are dozens of televisions around the room and all of them are tuned to various sports events going on."

"Oh," Gretchen said. "So The Kid, as you call him, has a gambling addiction where he is losing all his money, and he has to sit in his job, his sport, while the very things he is betting on play out around him."

"No wonder he's homeless and living in his car," I said.

Stan nodded. "He has lost all focus."

If this wasn't hopeless, I didn't know what was. But I didn't say that.

Chapter Four

"The standard way of dealing with an addiction," Gretchen said, "is to remove the addicted person from the environment causing the addiction."

Stan nodded.

"How long can The Kid be away from poker?" Gretchen asked Stan. "Will he lose his powers if he is away too long?"

"He will," Stan said, nodding. "But a few years won't make any difference if he needs to be away. Usually takes a decade or more for a superhero's powers to fade beyond rescue."

Gretchen nodded. "Can we jump to where he is and not be seen?"

I was impressed. Gretchen clearly had some ideas and was taking control of all this. She seemed to have gone from a young, afraid kid to a professional woman in a matter of seconds.

Patty glanced at me and smiled.

"We can," Stan said. "Might not be pretty, though."

A moment later we were in a small casino on the east coast. The place smelled of mold and bad air-conditioning and had a few dozen people sitting at some older slots, all chain-smoking. The casino had a three-table poker nook off to one side with no one sitting at the tables.

The Kid, his clothes rumpled and his hair far longer than the last time I saw him, sat in the small sports book, watching an arena football game.

"Can he see us at all?" Gretchen asked her father. "Or sense us here?"

Stan shook his head. "I have us a half turn out of the normal world, like Poker Boy's office. The Kid can't see or hear us."

"Wow, nifty skill," I said to Stan. "That on the agenda to teach me at some point?"

"Got a hunch you already know how to do it," Stan said while staring at The Kid.

I liked the sound of that.

As Gretchen moved around to get in front of The Kid, I watched Stan.

I could tell that The Kid failing like this was really hurting Stan more than he wanted to ever let on.

"He's very handsome under all the dirty clothes and lack of a haircut," Gretchen said.

"He is," Patty said.

Stan and I both said nothing to that.

Gretchen kept staring at The Kid, at one point kneeling down in front of him to look up into his eyes.

"He is tortured," she said, her voice sad.

Gretchen then looked up at her father. "Do you know of a tropical island somewhere where The Kid and I can go and be isolated, yet live comfortably? The island can't have television or any kind of gambling and ideally no other people around."

Stan nodded. "I am sure I can find a place."

Gretchen nodded, standing and looking around the tired, small casino as she moved back over to stand beside her father.

She looked at me and Patty, then at her father. "He has no hope of even living if he stays in this environment."

All three of us nodded to that. We knew that, had seen the signs of problem gambling more times than any of us wanted to admit. The Kid had them all.

Gretchen looked at me. "Can we go back to your office and plan this all out?"

I nodded and a moment later I had us all back in our spots in the booth.

Gretchen first looked at her father. "We need the island and we need it yesterday. By my reading on The Kid, if he loses whatever he is betting on tonight, he might not live to the morning. And he will never call for help."

"Oh, shit," Stan said. "I'll be back as soon as I have something arranged."

Stan vanished and Gretchen, now showing more power and control than anyone her age should have the right to show, said to us. "Patty, can you find him new clothes. Beach clothes and everything he is going to need to survive for a while on a warm island. Including bathroom gear and such."

"I'll have two suitcases packed and here waiting in one hour," Patty said.

"Bring one set of clothes for The Kid to wear as well.

Patty nodded and vanished.

Gretchen turned to me. "I'm going to go talk to my boss, tell her what I am doing, get some check-in plans worked out, see if I am missing anything on this start."

I nodded. "Sounds sensible. What can I do?"

"I need you to go get him before he either wins or loses that bet, take him to a major hotel suite, toss away his clothes and everything he has on him, and make him shower a few times before Patty gets there with clothes."

I nodded. I didn't much like my part in this, but I knew I could control The Kid if I had to. And with luck, I wouldn't have to.

At that, Gretchen vanished, leaving me sitting alone in the booth.

I took a deep breath and then said to myself, "Let's get this done."

First I jumped to the MGM Grand and talked to Patty's boss and got a suite paid for.

Then, with a deep breath, I jumped back to The Kid in

the sad excuse for a casino. He hadn't moved, and the game he must have had a bet on was still going on. His eyes were glassy.

I walked up to him and said, "Hi, Kid."

He jumped. If he had been at full focus and power, I never would have been able to surprise him.

"Things not going well I see," I said.

He shrugged. "I've been worse."

"Actually," I said, "I think you'll look back on this, if you live, and call this your worst moment."

At that I jumped the two of us to the MGM Grand suite I had rented.

"Wait! What are you doing?"

"Trying to save your life," I said.

I then jumped him, without his clothes, into the shower.

"Stay in there," I shouted to him, "until you don't smell like the inside of a sewer."

I teleported his clothes to the city landfill as I heard the water turn on.

He had not learned how to teleport, so he was trapped by me and he knew it.

In his condition, it was unlikely he even cared.

And that just made me sad. He had been a great poker player, could have been one of the best in the world.

But the control he felt in poker didn't give him the needed adrenaline feel he got from winning something out of his control.

And that need for the thrill and the real risk had driven him down to this place.

I was just glad Stan had been paying attention. It's always the worst when someone dies from an addiction and not even their closest friends knew of the problem or had time to even try to help.

That happens more than I wanted to think about.

Chapter Five

Patty brought The Kid some clothes and after he was dressed, I jumped the three of us back to my office.

Stan sat there in the booth with Gretchen.

The Kid just shook his head and stared at the floor.

Gretchen introduced herself, smiling and The Kid introduced himself as Steve.

"I thought you were called The Kid?" Gretchen asked.

The Kid nodded and sat down in a chair facing the booth. "Steve was my real name. I don't much feel like The Kid at the moment."

"So you know you have a leak," Stan said to The Kid.

The Kid took a deep breath and nodded. "Turned into a bad one I couldn't seem to get out of, even though I knew what was happening and knew better."

Stan nodded and since he was The Kid's boss, we let him go on.

"What do you suggest we do about this gambling addiction problem?" Stan asked.

The Kid jerked at that. It was one thing to call it a "leak" that poker players understood. Calling it by what it really was clearly hurt The Kid.

"I honestly don't know," he said, his eyes down. "I assume I am fired."

"No, not yet," Stan said. "We're going to give you a chance to control this, put it into your past."

The kid looked up at Stan, surprised.

I could see a slight glimmering of hope in his eyes.

It felt almost pathetic.

Stan went on. "Gretchen is my daughter and a trained expert in all sorts of psychological issues. She is a superhero in that area, actually."

The Kid looked at Gretchen again and nodded, clearly embarrassed.

"Here is what is going to happen," Stan said. "We are going to put you and Gretchen on a remote small island, without television, cards, or anyone else for that matter."

Again The Kid started.

Stan went on. "You are going to exercise, rest, and work with Gretchen on this issue until the two of you dig it out and she tells me you can come back to work without worry of a leak again. She will be reporting in to me every day."

The Kid looked at Gretchen, then at Stan. "You both would do that for me?"

"We will do that gladly," Stan said, his voice about as firm as I had ever heard it. "But let me be clear. This will not be easy, and you have the ability to ask to leave at any point. But if you leave one minute before Gretchen tells me you are ready, I will fire you and remove your powers and you will never see any of us again. Are we understood?"

The Kid swallowed and nodded. "I understand. And thank you."

"Thank me when my daughter says you are ready and not one moment before," Stan said.

Then Stan nodded to Gretchen and she and The Kid vanished, along with the suitcases that had been sitting near the booth.

Stan seemed to slump in the booth and at that moment Madge came in carrying fresh fries and new milkshakes.

"I figured after that," she said, her voice solemn, "you all could use a little something."

"Sorry you had to hear that, Madge," Stan said.

Madge put down the food and shrugged. "My first husband was a long time ago. He was sick like that kid is sick and he died from it. That's just the way it goes. I hope you all can save The Kid, but honestly, I think you have a better chance of saving the world from aliens again."

With that she turned and left.

"She's right," Stan said, shaking his head.

"But people are saved from this sickness," Patty said.

I didn't say anything, but I had never heard of a poker player recovering from this and still playing poker.

And I had a hunch Stan hadn't either. What made a great poker player was often what caused this kind of problem.

As Stan had told me early on, sometimes you save people and sometimes you just can't. I had lost my share of people I had tried to save over the years. It always had a sick, sinking feeling about it when it happened.

A helpless feeling.

I was feeling it right at that moment.

Two weeks later, as we were all eating lunch in my office, Gretchen appeared and sat down next to her father. She looked tan under her white blouse and jeans and seemed disgusted.

She turned to her father. "The Kid, as he is now calling himself again, declared himself cured and wanted to be dropped at a casino in New York."

"Shit," Stan said. "Just shit."

An instant later Stan vanished.

He and I had talked about what he would do if this happened. He would go to Laverne and they would strip The Kid of any memory of being a superhero and all his powers.

I felt sick to my stomach. Just sick.

Patty leaned her head on my shoulder, which made me feel a little better. But not much, since she was feeling as bad as I was.

Madge had appeared and slid a milkshake in front of

Gretchen, then patted her on the shoulder and said she was sorry. "It had been worth the try."

Gretchen shrugged. "I did everything I could, but Steve has one fatal flaw that he never wanted to address."

"Can I ask what that was?" I didn't know if I was stepping over bounds or not.

Gretchen shrugged. "Doesn't matter now. His flaw was his ego. He actually believed he could beat any bet or game he set his mind to. He just flat thought he was the greatest and there wasn't a bet he couldn't take on and eventually win."

I felt that way at a poker table, but never one step beyond a poker table. No wonder The Kid had a leak.

Stan appeared again, sitting next to his daughter. "It's done. The Kid has no memory of any of us, or any superpowers. All stripped away."

Silence filled the office.

Outside, the Vegas sky was blue, the day a wonderful day.

Inside the office, the day was shitty. We had given our best to try and save someone and just failed.

It was that simple.

And that hard.

We got a report eight months later that he had been found dead in his car in Florida, penniless and homeless.

He had leaked away an entire life.

None of us were surprised at the news.

GODS HAVE HISTORY

Chapter One

I had learned a long time ago for me, meaning about five years or so, that there was no such thing as perfect answers.

Every answer I seemed to get over the years to my often-stupid questions seemed to have more than one answer. Or worse yet, the answer was shaded in "it depends" which is a color that seems to be more like a cloud of mist.

Today, the question I had asked of Patty and Stan seemed to be getting a combination of "it depends" and more than one answer.

A double whammy.

Patty Ledgerwood, aka Front Desk Girl worked as a superhero in the hotel and lodging part of the world. Stan, my direct boss, was the God of Poker. As Poker Boy, a superhero,

I worked for him and made my living playing poker when not running around saving people or the entire planet.

But even though Stan was my boss, basically I ran the team and he was part of the team. It was a complicated relationship, but we both seemed to be just fine with it. I knew he was the boss, he understood I was, at times, so new to this business of gods and superheroes, that I had no idea what was happening.

I was just good at questions that seemed to poke others into action and thus save the world from whatever evil was threatening it at the moment.

Patty and Stan and I were sitting in the big diner booth in the center of my invisible floating office over Las Vegas. Besides a few chairs, the booth was the only furniture in the big square glass room. The booth looked like I had lifted it from a 1950s diner.

The walls of my office were perfectly clear and I had put a wood railing about belt high all the way around the room so I didn't feel like I might fall off the floor at any moment.

Patty, who had her long brown hair pulled back and was wearing a wonderful white blouse and jeans instead of her normal MGM Grand front desk uniform, sat beside me. She had brown eyes that could hold me frozen it seemed and her touch actually could calm me. That was one of her many superpowers.

She had a day off and after lunch we were planning on jumping to our new home that was being built in the Oregon

Coastal Range to see how things were moving along. And then we planned on having a nice dinner in Portland at a restaurant we both loved there before jumping back here for a movie and other activities that often happened on date night.

Stan had on a button-down gray sweater, gray slacks, and loafers. His hair was cut short and he was the most forget-table-looking person I had ever met. He took the "not be noticed" approach to poker while I had always taken the more flamboyant approach by wearing a black fedora-like hat and a black leather coat all the time.

I considered that coat and hat my superhero costume. Not sure if it actually helped me, but it sure felt like it did at times. And besides, I liked it.

The question I had asked had been simple, or so I thought. "When did the gods actually start. And how?"

I was really tired of always being surprised by my lack of knowledge of the thousands of gods and more thousands of other superheroes that roamed the planet taking care of every tiny niche of human life. In fact, right now we were waiting for milkshakes and burgers to be brought to us by Madge, who owned a real diner in downtown Vegas where my team used to meet before we got this office. Madge was a superhero in the food service area.

Also, it seemed that at five years, I was one of the youngest of all superheroes working. I had been an orphan growing up, so I had no idea who birthed a superhero kid. Not a clue.

Superheroes basically stopped aging in their late twenties

and could live forever, from what I understand. I had no idea how old exactly Patty was, but I know it was hundreds and hundreds of years older than me.

I would like to say that being in love with an older woman didn't bother me, and most of the time it didn't. But every so often she would reveal a part of her past from hundreds of years earlier and I would feel pretty darned inadequate.

I usually got over it quickly when she kissed me. More than likely another one of her superpowers. I didn't mind at all.

So my question about the origin of the gods had been with the idea that Patty and Stan could help me start to fill in some knowledge gaps.

But Stan had just laughed and said, "Not really sure, to be honest."

Stan was a master at avoiding a direct answer and that felt like a real avoidance. I knew Stan had been alive in the Atlantis days. We had even rescued his two missing daughters from that time. So he had to have had some idea.

Patty had smiled at me. "Why would that matter?"

"So you know?" I asked her.

"I honestly don't," she said.

Stan shrugged.

At that point, Madge came up carrying a cheeseburger basket with fries for Stan and one for me and Patty to split.

She also had a vanilla milkshake for Stan and one for me and Patty. The milkshakes were so huge and rich and wonderful that Patty and I were lucky to even get through half of one each.

Stan always managed to finish one of his own.

The cheeseburger and fries smelled wonderful and Patty grabbed the salt shaker to salt the fries.

"Madge," I said, "Do you know the origin of the gods and superheroes? About when they started and how?"

She laughed. "Do I look that old to you?"

"Don't answer that," Patty said to me, laughing.

"Just thought I would try to learn a little history today is all," I said, raising my hands in surrender.

"I honestly have no idea," Madge said, laughing, as she vanished into the portal leading back down to her diner.

Now I was really puzzled. I glanced at Stan. "Do you think Ben could join us for lunch?"

"You're not going to let this go, are you?" Stan asked, staring at me to try to get a read on me.

"Do I ever let anything go?" I asked.

Both he and Patty laughed and then he vanished.

I turned to Patty as she started to pick up her half of the cheeseburger. "You honestly don't know?"

"I don't," she said. "Honestly, until you asked the question, never thought about it."

She bit into her half of the cheeseburger as my warning bells in the back of my head started to go off.

Patty didn't know.

Stan didn't know or wouldn't say.

Madge didn't know.

I had a hunch that I had just stuck my finger into a large hornet's nest and didn't even know it.

Typical for me and my stupid questions.

Just damn typical.

CHAPTER TWO

Stan appeared about one minute later with Ben, the oldest superhero I had ever met, at least in looks.

Ben looked like a college professor, with bifocal glasses and a tweed jacket and vest that he seemed to always wear. He had been the god of lamplighters, but Stan and I had found him one day, almost faded completely away and got him to move to be a god in the books and library area. That had perked him back up and he was happy.

It seems that for centuries and centuries, he read everything he could, including the entire library of Alexandria, which was now part of the Library of Atlantis. And he remembered everything he had read.

So he had become the history of my team, the person we turned to when information from the past might save our lives. Amazing how often it did.

"Stan tells me you are trying to learn some history," Ben said, sliding into the booth next to Stan. "As I have offered in the past, I am always willing to help."

"I appreciate that," I said, wiping my mouth of any stray ketchup from the burger. "My question seemed simple, but turns out it's not. Basically I was curious as to how the gods and superheroes started. And how we became immortal and all that."

Patty and Stan and I all watched Ben as his face went white.

Now some major alarm bells were going off in my head. I had really stumbled into it now.

Stan glanced at me, raised an eyebrow. He was surprised as well and more than likely feeling the same worry.

Damn, it had been a nice lunch and I had gone and ruined it by my stupid questions.

Ben took a deep breath and turned to Stan. "I think we need to talk with Laverne."

Now both of Stan's eyebrows went up and he nodded, put down the fry he had been about to eat and the two of them vanished.

Laverne was the most powerful god working right now. She was Lady Luck herself. The more I learned about her, the more powerful I understood she actually was.

"Got any idea what I just caused?" I asked Patty.

She just shook her head. "Maybe there's a reason I didn't know the answer to your question."

"My little voice is telling me it's not a good reason," I said.

"It's not a bad reason either," Laverne said as she and Stan and Ben appeared.

Ben and Stan slid back into the booth and Laverne pulled up a chair at the end of the booth and took one of Stan's fries.

Laverne had on a gray silk suit with a blue blouse under it. She had her long hair pulled back and tied off, making her classic beauty look stark and very powerful.

"I have put a shield around this office so that no one, and I mean no one, can hear what I am about to tell you four."

Suddenly I wished I had not taken as many bites of the cheeseburger as I had.

"Ben knows this," Laverne said, "and since I trust you three with the world's life at times, I figured I can trust you with this bit of history."

I nodded thanks.

"So you want to know where and how the gods and superheroes started?" Laverne asked, turning to face me.

"It seemed like a simple question," I said. "Appears it is not."

"Our official history is, of course, fairly well known," Laverne said. "We fought on the side of the elves and the dwarves to defeat the Titans, who were trying to control and dominate the world."

I nodded. "So most of the textbook stuff has truth in it?"

"It does," Laverne said. "We did not expect to be worshipped after the win and didn't much like it, to be honest, which is why we quickly went underground and our history became myths, including the god and superhero parts."

I nodded at that. That much I understood. They were all called gods, but no god I had ever met actually acted like one. They just all had powers.

"So we evolved on the planet before that?" I asked.

She shook her head. "No race that now lives on this planet originated here."

I started to open my mouth and then what she had said sunk in and I shut it.

"Even the Silicon Suckers at one point in the far distant past came here from other worlds in this galaxy," Ben said. "The Titans did as well. So did dwarves and elves, and humans and gods. The war with the Titans did not start on this planet and did not end here either."

"Is it over?" Patty asked.

"For the moment," Laverne said.

Oh, great, just great.

Stan had lost his entire poker face and was just staring at Laverne. Ben was watching Laverne, taking his lead from her, clearly.

Beside me, Patty was breathing in a slow, shallow fashion, clearly upset.

"So we are all aliens?" I asked.

"Not after forty thousand years here on the planet," Laverne said, laughing. "I think we can all be called locals just fine. Just as the Silicon Suckers and the dwarves and elves are."

"Oh," was all I could think to say.

And honestly, that felt intelligent to me at that moment.

Chapter Three

Laverne looked at all four of us and smiled. "Hard to imagine, isn't it?"

"Very," Patty said.

Imagining was the least of my issues at the moment. I just wanted to get my brain working to even have a thought that made sense.

"There is something I need to show you all," Laverne said.

A moment later I found myself standing next to Patty in a dark space that smelled faintly of cleaner.

The lights came up slowly until the massive space was bright with light. What was around me made no sense at all to my poor poker brain. There were a good fifty chairs at what looked to be some sort of futuristic computer station.

All the stations were coming to life as well, showing readings in a language that looked like something from Egypt to me.

The gigantic room had a high, domed ceiling and was layered in half circles all facing a massive front wall that was blank. Most of the panels and chairs were around the walls on the top half circle.

There was a secondary circle of stations on a slightly lower level and then down in the center was a station with four chairs. Two big ones sort of melded together and one on each side of the big one.

Everything seemed to be focused on the massive blank wall that filled a third of the room in front of the lower level.

It looked like a control room for a massive power station or something.

"This is the bridge of our ship, *Olympus*," Laverne said.

Ship! What kind of ship?

Again my poor brain was going back into lockdown. For being a hero who had helped save the world a bunch of times, I was sure having trouble today just keeping it together.

"Welcome back," Chairman," a soft, female computer voice said. "Welcome Commander."

The huge screen in front of the massive room came alive, but it showed nothing but a faint light.

"It is good to be back," Laverne said.

"Agreed," Ben said.

Laverne was called Chairman and Ben had been a commander. Confused didn't even begin to describe how I was feeling. Numb seemed to be closer to accurate.

"Status of *Olympus?*" Laverne asked.

"All systems are active and on standby," the computer voice said. "All are tested regularly and any issues repaired."

"Good," Laverne said.

"Any crew on board at this point?" Ben asked.

"None of the crew has returned in over seven hundred years planet time," the ship said.

Laverne nodded. "Please recognize these three new arrivals as official members of the crew."

"Understood," the big ship said. "Welcome."

I think my brain got my body to say "Thank you."

Patty did the same.

Stan just nodded.

"Olympus," Laverne said, "Can you give us an image of space outside this ship on the big screen please, aimed sunward?"

So we were on a spaceship? In space.

Good to know.

It sure didn't feel like I thought space would feel.

A massive image of stars spread out over the screen. Beautiful didn't begin to describe it. Millions and millions of stars filled that screen.

"Oh, my," Patty said.

"Please indicate the sun we orbit," Laverne said.

A line was drawn around one tiny star that looked only slightly brighter than the others. Wow, we were a long, long ways out in space if that was the sun.

Laverne turned to the three of us. "We are in an orbit just

outside the system where Earth lives. The ship is hidden among debris here and made to look like a small moon on the outside. It is completely shielded.

"Why?" Patty asked a half second before I could. "If you have this ship here, why didn't you just move on? Or go home. Or whatever?"

"Our home has always been *Olympus,*" Laverne said, a touch of pride in her voice. "This ship is about the same size as the Earth moon and can hold hundreds of thousands at any given point."

"Were you born on this ship?" I asked Laverne.

She shook her head. "I was born in a distant galaxy and recruited with my husband to have the honor to be the Chairman of this wonderful ship. *Olympus* was my home for sixty thousand years before we arrived here through a series of accidents."

"So *Olympus* is working?" I asked.

"I am working, Poker Boy," the ship's voice said.

"We chose to stay and live on the planet," Ben said. "At least for a time."

A time? I had a hunch that forty thousand years was more than the time they had planned to start.

"Why?" I asked.

"Because we found aliens," Laverne said. "Three different races, actually, all growing and expanding in the same galaxy. Titans, Elves and Dwarves, and Silicon Suckers."

"Normally," Ben said, "it was rare to find even one alien race in the billions of worlds in a galaxy. We did not mingle with alien races in any way. We just gave the galaxy a wide pass and moved on. The universe is a very empty place out there. Alien races are very rare and seldom survive, let alone move between stars as the three in this galaxy have done."

"But this one planet and a dozen others, through complete error and circumstance, we had already seeded with humans in this galaxy," Laverne said. "Some of our seeder ships got out ahead of us and this galaxy was not well scouted, clearly."

"Seeder ships?" Patty asked, again a second before my brain could ask the same question.

"That was the *Olympus* mission," Laverne said. "To seed human cultures through the different galaxies."

"So once we discovered the mistake, we decided to stop," Ben said, "pull in all our ships, and go into hiding here and help the planets with humans survive."

"And thanks to this team," Laverne said, indicating me and Patty and Stan, "We are continuing to do that on the last human planet left in this galaxy."

"What happened to the others?" Stan asked.

"We lost many battles in the war," Laverne said.

There was no chance in hell I was going to ask more about that.

"Do you see a time when many of you will return to *Olympus* and move on?" Patty asked.

Laverne nodded. "At some point, in the distant future, we hope to do just that. And with many new crew members."

Laverne looked at the three of us. "But first we need to

keep this planet, this last human world in this galaxy, safe for as long as we can."

That much I understood.

Saving the world made sense to me. Spaceships on the other hand were another matter altogether.

Laverne turned. "*Olympus*, would you please ask my husband to join me. We need to check in with Chairman Wade if it has been seven hundred years."

"I will be glad to, Chairman," *Olympus* said.

Laverne turned to me. "Now, we have answered the question as to our origin. But you three will need to keep it to yourselves. Most of the new gods and superheroes do not know of *Olympus* yet."

I nodded, completely understanding. "May we visit *Olympus* again to get a tour, if that would be all right with *Olympus*?"

"Yes, please," Patty said.

Stan nodded.

"I would be honored," *Olympus* said. "If the Chairman gives permission."

"They will always have my permission," Laverne said.

I nodded to Laverne. "Thank you for being honest with us."

She nodded and a moment later I was sitting next to Patty in the booth in my floating office over Las Vegas.

My half-eaten part of our cheeseburger still actually looked good.

Ben was smiling, staring at all of us.

Stan just shook his head and dug into his remaining fries and cheeseburger. I hoped someday to be that calm and collected about world-shattering news as Stan was.

"Thank you," I said to Ben.

"For exactly what?" he asked, smiling.

"For answering what seemed to be a silly question with respect."

"Our history should always be respected," he said. "Here and on *Olympus*."

"There is a lot to learn," I said.

"We have time," Ben said, smiling.

I nodded and went back to working on my cheeseburger. Before today I had thought the history here on Earth of the gods and superheroes was complex and a lot to learn. Now I also had thousands of years of *Olympus* history as well to try to figure out.

I was going to need a lot of years.

More than I could probably imagine at the moment.

A whole lot more.

For The Balance Of
A Heart

CHAPTER ONE

I always figured that when Lady Luck needed a favor from me, things had to be really, really bad.

Laverne, aka Lady Luck, appeared a little after noon on a Friday. My entire team was in my new office eating take-out Chinese and talking about our plans for the weekend. I had a poker tournament I hoped to play in later in the evening at the Bellagio and Patty Ledegerwood, aka Front Desk Girl, my sidekick and girlfriend, had to work swing at the MGM Grand Hotel front desk.

In other words, a pretty standard weekend night for us.

Then Lady Luck appeared.

When that happens, normal becomes a laughing matter.

Laverne had on her standard business casual gray pantsuit. Her dark hair was pulled so tight into a bun on the top of her head that it had to hurt. Her eyes looked neutral as they always did. Lady Luck seldom showed anyone any emotion and it was always impossible to get a read on what she was thinking.

She looked around my new office and smiled and then nodded. "Original."

I thought that meant she liked my new office layout. At least I hoped that was what she meant.

She glanced at Stan, the God of Poker who was trying to choke down the remains of a spring role. "Good job."

Stan, who had on his standard gray cardigan sweater and gray slacks, only nodded. Compliments from Lady Luck herself were rare and Stan knew that. The expression on his face and in his dark eyes never changed.

At times I couldn't believe my new office, or the fact that a superhero poker player like me even had an office. But I did, and it was invisible and floated above the city of Las Vegas, about a thousand feet above the MGM Grand Casino and Hotel.

I doubted I would ever get used to how amazing that was.

Since Patty worked at the MGM Grand, I figured directly above the MGM Grand just seemed like a great place to anchor the office. Besides, since I got a lot of my superhero power from casinos funneled through my black leather coat and Fedora-like hat, being parked over a major casino never hurt.

And I seldom took off my coat and hat. Even now over a Chinese lunch that was about to get very cold.

The office in this spot also allowed for a great view of all of Las Vegas and the surrounding mountains and desert since all four walls were glass and perfectly clear. At first that had scared me so much I stayed to the center of the room. Finally, after a day of almost crawling around the room on my hands and knees for fear of falling off the edge of my office tile floor, I had decided to put in a wooden rail about a foot wide and waist-high across the glass. On all four walls. That helped. I now could actually go to the edges of my own office and look down.

Compared to normal offices, mine really wasn't much of an office. No desk, no couches, no pictures or awards hanging on the glass walls. The entire center of the square office was filled with a large, oblong wooden booth. It was an exact replica of the booth in the Diner Restaurant from downtown Las Vegas where we had all met for the last couple of years.

Plastic-covered booth seats and a scarred tabletop made it feel real. Bottles of ketchup and mustard sat next to the salt and pepper and a pile of white paper napkins in the center.

Every detail was the same as in the Diner.

In other words, my nifty new office was nothing more than a hunk of tile floor and a diner booth floating in the air over a major casino. I liked it.

So did the rest of the team, or so they had said.

The booth was large enough to handle the six members of my team. There were two or three extra chairs in the room that visitors could pull up to the end of the booth and a couple of lawn chairs in one corner where Patty and I could just sit and stare out at the city and the mountains.

I'd only had this office for a week and I was starting to love sitting in those lawn chairs in the evenings before sunset.

Lady Luck turned around, grabbed a chair and pulled it toward the end of the booth where we were all sitting. It had been Lady Luck herself who had suggested that Stan, my boss and the God of Poker, teach me how to build and secure a floating office for me and my team.

Over the last few years my team had saved the world more times than I wanted to count, so it seemed like a great idea to me and it was turning out to be just that. But while I was building it, I hadn't been so sure.

It had taken two very long days and just about every ounce of energy I had, even with Stan helping, to put it all together and get it secured somehow in its floating and invisible location. But now it took no energy at all for me to keep it there.

Stan tried to explain to me how that worked, but I flat didn't understand a word he said. I figured there had to be some things only the gods could or should know. Since I was only a lowly superhero in the gambling universe, I wasn't meant to know what we had just done or how it even worked. Honestly, I was fine with that, as long as the office stayed in the air and we could go and come from it.

Lady Luck pulled the chair to the table and sat down. Then she sampled a bite of an extra spring roll and nodded. The food was from a restaurant called Larry's Chinese Place just off The Strip. The locals knew it was the best in town.

My entire team was there, plus Stan. I could tell they were

all as shocked by Lady Luck's action as I felt. One of the most powerful gods in the universe just didn't join a bunch of superheroes and a poker god for lunch.

The Smoke and Screamer both eased away from her on the left side of the booth. The Smoke was basically a werewolf who could walk through walls. He stood about my height at six foot, but had shoulders so large it made him seem shorter. His most striking feature was his deep blue eyes.

Screamer was shorter than me and usually just wore Las Vegas tourist clothes like bright shirts and ugly shorts. He worked for the law enforcement side of the gods and seemed far, far harder than he actually was.

Madge, the food-service-superhero waitress who always wore a too-tight pink diner uniform and owned and ran the Diner, had been sitting on the end on the right side. She now stood and moved to a position behind the booth facing Lady Luck and behind Stan, who sat in the middle.

Patty and I moved closer to Lady Luck on the right side, taking up some of the room left by Madge.

No one said a word and the smell from the Chinese food filling the middle of the table wasn't helping my stomach any. Since my team covered five different branches of the gods, we were unusual, but I just never expected Lady Luck to join us for anything.

"Poker Boy," Laverne said, looking at me. Then she looked at Stan. "Everyone, I need a personal favor."

Now I really, really, really wished I hadn't just eaten that last piece of sweet-and-sour chicken. Lady Luck never asked for personal favors. She had been alive for longer than any written history. Civilizations over the centuries had come and gone, but Lady Luck had lived through them all. So her asking us for a personal favor had to mean things were really, really bad.

"Anything," I managed to say. Stan only nodded and even though he was the God of Poker with the best poker face I had ever seen, I could tell he was too surprised to even speak.

Everyone else nodded slightly, clearly too stunned to dare move much.

"Thank you," she said. Then she took a deep breath. "I need you to find Helen, my daughter."

I was fairly certain at that moment I had stopped breathing.

Lady Luck had just told me she had a daughter. I had thought I was starting to get a grip on all the different gods and superheroes and who worked for whom and who hated whom. But now it was clear there was still a great deal I didn't know about all the whos and whoms of the world of gods.

"Do you know where she was last seen?" Stan asked.

Thank heavens Stan knew about Lady Luck having a daughter and was managing to keep his wits about him. That was the difference between a god and a bunch of superheroes. He'd been alive a lot longer and could roll better with very, very strange requests.

And even better, he could explain it all to us after she left.

"Helen is somewhere here in Las Vegas," Lady Luck said.

"And I have no idea what she is doing or why she has vanished. I can't even sense her."

"How long has she been gone?" I managed to ask, at least trying to sound logical and in control and leader-like. Thankfully, my voice didn't squeak.

"About twelve minutes now," Laverne said, clearly serious. "I am very worried."

She started to take another bite from the spring roll, then changed her mind and pushed it away.

"We'll do our best," Stan said.

"Thank you," Lady Luck said, nodding. "I know you will."

With that she vanished, leaving the chair empty at the end of the booth.

I stared at the empty chair for what seemed like hours, but it must have only been a few seconds. Then I turned back to the stunned faces of my team.

"Wow," Madge said from behind Stan. "The Queen of Hearts has gone missing. Imagine that."

Now all I could do was stare at Madge.

She just shrugged. "I'll get some milkshakes for everyone if someone gets rid of all that dead food. Looks like we got some planning to do."

With that she turned and vanished. I had put in an invisible door right behind the booth—with Stan's help—that allowed Madge and most of the team to move back and forth between the real diner in downtown Las Vegas and my office.

I also put a door from my office to Patty's apartment so

Patty could be in the office as much as she liked as well, even when I wasn't here. I was the only member of the team besides Stan who knew how to teleport.

Across from me in the booth, The Smoke, a part-human, part-wolf superhero in the world of animals, looked completely shocked, his blue eyes wider than normal by a ways. That was going some.

Beside him, Screamer just looked down at the pile of uneaten Chinese food and shook his head. Screamer worked under the gods of law enforcement and his superpower was the ability to take thoughts from one person and put them in another person's head. He had seen more than I ever wanted to imagine and yet he seemed bothered by this.

I honestly couldn't believe what had just happened either.

Lady Luck had a daughter, who was missing, and Lady Luck had come to us to find her.

That did not bode well for anyone involved.

I looked out over the city of Las Vegas. Helen, the Queen of Hearts, was out there somewhere. And up until a moment ago, I didn't even know she existed beyond the faces of the cards I played poker with.

Had she been the one to pose for those early cards? Or was that just her nickname? So many questions.

In the distance, a Southwest airliner turned for final approach to McCarran Airport. Sometimes a plane landing at the airport got a little too close to this invisible office for comfort, but Stan assured me that a plane could hit the office and it would go right through and no one would notice.

Something about the office and everyone in it being a half-turn out of normal time and space.

Again I didn't understand what he meant, but I was fairly certain I didn't want to be in the office the day a plane passed through it.

I was drifting. I had to get focused.

I turned to Stan who was just sitting staring out over the countryside as well, his eyes blank.

Beside me, Patty took my hand and squeezed it, sending waves of comfort and calm through me. She worked under the Gods of Hospitality. Calming people was one of her many superpowers. I loved it.

"Stan, can you tell us about Helen? And why Madge called her the Queen of Hearts?"

"Because for centuries, even before I was born, which was before Atlantis, she has been called that," Stan said. "Her beauty is legendary. Red hair, very tall, and a temper when unleashed that could level a city."

"And she's been gone now for thirteen or so minutes?" I asked. "How does Laverne know that?"

Stan shrugged. "Some sort of connection, a family bond, at a level I am not familiar with."

"And that clearly was broken," I said.

Stan nodded. "I can't sense her either."

I sat back and looked out at the view. I had no idea where to even start on this problem. And that scared me a lot.

"We're missing a lot of information here," Screamer said.

"First off, who would have the power to cut the link between Lady Luck and her daughter?"

"Good question," I said. "Can't be many people I would imagine."

"Unless Helen did it herself," The Smoke said in his level, deep voice.

I glanced at Stan who sat calmly, not saying anything.

"Stan?" I asked. "You know who could do this, don't you?"

Stan nodded, but said nothing. Instead he made all the food on the table just vanish with a simple wave of his hand, leaving the scarred wood top as clean as if Madge had spent an hour wiping it down. I had no idea where he sent it all.

"Stan?" I pushed.

He looked up and seemed almost afraid to say what he was about to say. And when a god was afraid to say something, it couldn't be good.

Finally he put both hands on the table and looked first at Patty, then at me. "There is only one person who could break the link between Laverne and Helen purposefully."

"That's going to make the search a lot easier," Screamer said. "Who is it?"

"Laverne's husband," Stan said softly, again looking down at the table.

At that moment you could have heard a pin drop in my new floating office over Las Vegas. Nothing is ever supposed to be that quiet in or above Las Vegas.

CHAPTER TWO

I finally managed to choke out the most logical question we all had to be thinking, since we were all staring at Stan in shock. "Lady Luck is married?"

"Separated, actually," Stan said. "Centuries before I was born."

"His name?"

Stan shrugged. "He's gone by a lot of names over the centuries, just as Laverne has. Last I heard he liked Benny. Before that I think he went by Jonah. In Atlantis it was Belial."

"Evil one?" The Smoke asked, his voice almost a growl.

"Not really," Stan said. "Are you all familiar with the concept of Yin-Yang?"

I was slightly, only because of that circle with the two

black-and-white shapes inside it was sold as trinkets all over Vegas in just about every form.

Everyone else nodded and Stan went on.

Stan looked at me. "Ever wonder why you have as much bad luck as you have good over time?"

I honestly hadn't wondered that, or at least given it any meaning. I just knew it always balanced out in poker and skill always won out in the long run.

"Benny is the God of Bad Luck?" Screamer asked.

"Not really," Stan said, shaking his head. "Any more than Laverne is only good luck. But Benny and Laverne must both exist for the other to exist. Yin-yang. Dark and Light. Masculine and feminine. Only down through time the two sides of that have been confused when it comes to sex."

I was confused as well, but managed to ask "How?"

"Today the sunny, light side is called yang," Stan said, "and is also associated with masculine. That got flipped. Actually, when all this started, yin was masculine and in the shadow while yang was sunny and feminine. The key is that everything stays on the Golden Mean."

"The middle between two extremes," Patty said.

"That's right," Stan said.

I looked at my girlfriend in awe, then back at Stan. I had no doubt I could keep asking him questions and he could keep me confused for hours, And Patty could keep impressing me with her knowledge, but it seemed we had a task to do, so I needed to get that task in motion somehow.

"So, why would Benny cut off connections between Laverne and Helen?"

Stan shook his head. "I can't think of one reason. They both love Helen."

"So if she went to visit her father," Screamer asked, "where would she go?"

"He lives right here," Stan said. "You don't see him out much. He has a walled compound over near the university. He mostly stays to the dark side."

"And we live on the sunny side?" I asked.

Stan pointed at the clear blue sky around the booth.

"Yin-Yang," The Smoke said, his voice very soft as if he understood.

I honestly didn't, and I had no doubt Patty was going to have to help me understand later. But right at this moment, with Helen the Queen of Hearts missing, my understanding of ancient philosophy and aspects of how the gods work didn't much matter. I hoped there would be time to learn it all. For some reason, this problem felt world-ending serious and I had no idea why.

"Would crossing into the shadow side cause the connection to break?" I asked Stan.

"And if we crossed over there, what would happen?" Patty asked.

"And how could we cross over?" Screamer added.

Before Stan could answer, Madge appeared carrying milkshakes, the drink of choice for all of us when working on a case.

"You guys talking about going over into the shadow world?" Madge asked as she put the milkshakes in front of us.

Mine was vanilla with whipped cream stacked high. I really wasn't in the mood for a milkshake, but I forced myself to take a taste anyway. It was as wonderful as usual. I had no doubt that if this meeting kept going for another ten minutes, I would down the entire thing.

Patty nodded thanks to Madge for the milkshake, then answered her question. "We're just discussing if Helen crossing over would cause the connection between here and her mother to be broken."

"In some extreme areas of the shadow world, I suppose it might," Madge said. "But I honestly doubt it."

"I agree," Stan said.

Madge went on as she moved around the table delivering our shakes. "I've worked both sides of the line over the years. Not much purposely crosses the line because that line is always moving for everyone."

"She's right," Stan said. "Every action, every reaction by everyone moves the line for that person."

I was so confused I just wanted to slump down into the booth and cover my head. So I focused on the first question that came to mind.

"Madge, what's it like living on the other side of the line?"

"Exactly the same as here," she said, finishing putting out the milkshakes, napkins, straws and spoons for everyone. "You can't tell the difference, actually. It's the same world."

Banging my head on the table would probably do no

good, but I sure felt like doing that. And clearly Stan read me like a book.

"You ever sat at a poker table with a cheater?" Stan asked me.

"Sure," I said.

"How about a guy who couldn't buy a good card if his life depended on it, or played just a little too long and lost all his money."

"Sure," I said. "A normal table."

"They are living on the other side of the line," Stan said. "At least for their time at the table."

"So the shadow side isn't an actual place?" Screamer asked just slightly before I could.

"Yin-Yang," Madge said. "They both exist together and one could not exist without the other. Although I have to admit there is very little yin in this room. All yang."

"We all have our dark sides," The Smoke said.

Screamer nodded.

"Of course you do," Madge said. "There are no exceptions. But this group tends to not use the dark side without reason. And that's why I like to hang around with you all. I've spent far too much time solidly over on the other side of that line."

I looked at Madge with a brand new level of respect. Some day I was going to have to ask her a ton of questions about her past.

Patty just shook her head. "So if crossing the line would not normally block any connection between Helen and

Laverne, and visiting her father here in Las Vegas would not do that either, what would?"

I had the same question, but decided to ask it from another angle. I looked directly at Stan. "What exactly do you think Laverne is actually asking us to do?"

"Go into the tunnels," Stan said without looking at me.

"Not me," Madge said, turning and vanishing through the invisible door back to the Diner.

"I cannot go down there," The Smoke said, his eyes almost flashing anger.

"I understand," Stan said.

"Well, I don't understand much of anything we've been talking about," I said. "Laverne having a daughter, Laverne being married, yin-yang, and now tunnels. My head is starting to hurt. So would someone who understands these tunnels please explain them to me? Slowly."

Before anyone could say a word, Laverne appeared back in the chair at the end of the booth. She looked at Stan, her eyes intense. "You believe Helen might have actually gone down into the tunnels?"

"It would seem to be the only logical conclusion I'm afraid," Stan said.

"I came to the same conclusion," Lady Luck said and sat back, clearly shaken.

These tunnels, whatever they are, must be something very nasty to have Lady Luck act like that.

"I was so hoping it wasn't going to be that," she said. Then she took a deep breath and looked at Stan. "Explain to

Poker Boy and his team everything you can about the tunnels and I'll go talk with Helen's father. I'll see if he has any suggestions or has heard from Helen. I would imagine he's getting as worried as I am."

With that she vanished again.

The Smoke pushed to the end of the booth and stood. "I am sorry, I cannot help with the tunnels."

"I understand," Stan said.

I stared at The Smoke as he moved around the booth and vanished into the doorway to the Diner. I considered The Smoke one of the bravest I had ever met. And now he didn't seem to be afraid either. There was something else.

"You want to explain what just happened?" Screamer asked Stan before I could. There were only four of us left now to try to save Lady Luck's daughter.

"In a very ancient agreement between gods to end a war, The Smoke's people were banned from certain ancient cities back when the cities were inhabited. The agreement still holds even after hundreds of thousands of years."

"The tunnels are a part of an old city?" I asked.

"An ancient one," Stan said, nodding. "From the time of the Titans."

"I didn't know they were real," Patty said, saving me from asking yet another stupid question such as who were the Titans?

"Very real," Stan said. "Far before my time. They ruled this planet for almost two hundred thousand years, then one day they all suddenly vanished."

"Anyone know why?" I asked. "And I thought there were only a few of them. Why did they need cities?"

Stan shook his head. "The myths of their leaders is all that has survived. There were millions of Titans at one point in time. They are said to have ascended to a higher plain, or went into space, or got locked up by a powerful curse in a hidden prison."

"And the tunnels under Las Vegas is the remains of one of their cities?" Screamer asked.

"Actually," Stan said, "It is their main ancient city, their capital city. It is supposed to be completely preserved. It was buried by the gods who followed them into the position of ruling the planet. No one knows why. This area holds a great deal of unseen power, which is why so many of the gods live here, and why the city of Las Vegas even exists in this dry desert."

"And The Smoke can't go down there because his people got in a fight with the Titans?" Screamer asked.

Stan shook his head. "His area of the gods and a few others fought the Giants. In one battle they destroyed part of a Titan city and were forever banned from any Titan area ever since."

I took a deep breath and forced myself to focus through the thousand questions to stay squarely on the task Lady Luck had given us. "So Helen might have gone down there into an ancient protected city? Would that break the connection with her and her mother?"

"I'm assuming it would," Stan said. "The field surrounding that huge city is very powerful."

"How did she find her way in there?" Patty asked.

"Everyone knows how to get in," Stan said. "But no one has ever figured out how to get out."

"Wonderful," was all I could say.

Chapter Three

After a few more minutes of confusing me with more mythic history than I could begin to learn in a very long semester of college, I finally held up my hand.

"There is only one question we don't have an answer to," I said. "We don't know why Helen would go down there without a way back. What was she after?"

At that moment Lady Luck appeared. "She went after this."

In front of her and floating over the booth was an image of a golden key, turning slightly in the air. "Her father said she had been spending the last hundred years researching it and he says Helen thinks it is hidden in the old city."

As the key turned in the air over the table, it slowly transformed into a sneering, ugly man's face and then back into a golden key.

"That was one of the faces of Janus," Lady Luck said. "The key is one of his four faces. Some believe when combined with the other three keys, it will release the Titans to return to this time and space."

I had scooted away from the image of the floating key and finally Lady Luck snapped it out of existence.

"Why would she want to release the Titans?" Stan asked, his voice hushed.

I glanced at him. Clearly there was still a lot of very real history I had to learn.

Lady Luck sighed and dropped into the chair in front of the booth. "From what I understand, Helen has researched the Titans for centuries. Her father tells me she believes them to be an honorable race that have been unfairly imprisoned over time."

"And what do you believe?" I asked.

Lady Luck shook her head. "My beliefs are of little value now. We need to go into the old city and find Helen."

"No!" a deep voice said from just behind Lady Luck. "You cannot go into that city and you know it."

A small man, not more than five feet tall and as round as a basketball stepped up and looked into Lady Luck's eyes. If she hadn't been sitting down, she would have towered over him.

Now it was Stan's turn to push back as far as he could into the back of the booth.

Lady Luck said nothing.

After I stopped holding my breath for anyone talking to one of the most powerful gods in the world like a child, it dawned on me who the man was.

"Benny, I presume?" I asked.

He glanced at me. "Got it in one, Poker Boy."

Then he looked back at Laverne. "She's my daughter as well. But you and I both know you can't go in there after her. If you did not return, the world as we know it would collapse. We have both worked far too hard for that to happen. We must stay balanced. And to do that, you must stay here."

The silence in my little office felt like a heavy weight. Finally Benny looked away from his wife again and back at me, and then Stan.

"Find our daughter," he said softly. "We'll give you all the help we can from out here."

With that he and Laverne vanished.

I looked at the white faces of Screamer and Stan, then took Patty's hand in my own and squeezed it.

But all I could think about was that we were so screwed.

Chapter Four

For the next hour Stan explained to me and Patty and Screamer what "the tunnels" were. And how big they were supposed to be.

"But no one really knows what they can see from the doorways, since no one has ever returned after going in there."

Finally, I had to ask.

"So where is this entrance?"

Stan shook his head. "There is an old metal door right on the edge of Binion's Horseshoe Casino, about a hundred paces from Freemont Street down a side street."

"You're kidding," Screamer said.

"I'm not," Stan said. "No one notices it and you have to have some powers to open it. But all of you could do it."

"And no exit?" I asked.

"No one that I have heard of has gone in and come out again."

"Ever?" Patty asked.

Stan just shrugged, about as clear an answer as there was.

My stomach was so twisted into a knot around what was left of my Chinese food lunch, I couldn't even think of a response or another question.

"Well," Screamer said, finally, breaking into the silence, "let's hope we can find a way out once we are in there."

My mind was twisting again, struggling on what Screamer had just said. But I couldn't get it.

I turned to Screamer. "What you just said bothers me, but I can't put my finger on why."

"Bothers me as well," Screamer said, shaking his head. "For obvious reasons."

"Link us, would you?" I said, taking Patty's hand and then reaching my other hand across the booth between the empty milkshake glasses. "There's something I'm not seeing and I feel it might be the answer."

Screamer shrugged and glanced at Stan.

"I think I would only confuse the issue," Stan said. "Sometimes too much history and knowledge can hurt more than it can help."

I knew Stan was right, so Screamer reached over and touched my arm and suddenly he and Patty were both in my mind. We had done this sort of thing so many times over the years, it didn't even feel strange anymore.

It just felt familiar.

After only a few seconds, Screamer pulled his hand away from my arm and I was back alone in my own head.

Patty gave my hand a squeeze, but didn't let go, for which I was glad. Her touch kept me calm and thinking clearly, at least most of the time.

"See anything?" I asked Stan, then Patty.

"Something about the exit," Patty said.

"You were thinking we should find it first, before we go in."

Suddenly I knew the answer.

"That's exactly right," I said. "And I have an idea. I'll be right back."

I instantly teleported to the Diner.

Madge was scrubbing a counter far harder than it needed to be scrubbed. Clearly she was upset at herself for not wanting or being able to help.

"I need a thermos of hot chocolate," I said.

She looked at me and frowned. "Official or otherwise?"

"Official," I said. "How long?"

"Two minutes," she said, turning for the kitchen. "I'll bring it to you."

"Thanks." A moment later I was sitting next to Patty in the booth in my office.

And I was smiling. I knew how to find the exit, at least from this side.

"What was that all about?" Stan asked, looking as puzzled as the rest of my team.

"Call Laverne and Benny and I'll explain," I said.

"No need," Laverne said as she appeared again in the chair facing the booth. Benny was standing beside her and she still seemed taller than he was. "You think the exit is controlled by the Silicon Suckers?"

"I do," I said. "In fact, I'm convinced of it."

The Silicon Suckers were an ancient race of beings that lived in huge tunnels and caverns under desert regions of the planet. The gods, a long time ago, had negotiated a truce with them to keep humans and Silicon Suckers from fighting.

"How can you be so sure?" Benny asked, his voice deep and low and almost rumbling with power.

"There was a point when I was trying to save a superhero from the Keno side from her time with the Suckers. I had to watch her negotiate with the leader of the Silicon Suckers for an exchange of land for a number of thermos every month of hot chocolate."

"Strangest thing I had ever heard about," Benny said, shaking his head.

"During the negotiation, the leader of the Silicon Suckers floated a map in the air of the land around Las Vegas, showing what humans controlled and what they controlled. There was a giant round area under the city of Las Vegas that had neither human or Silicon Sucker color on it. At the time, I assumed it was that way because it was under the city and no one cared."

"The ancient city," Laverne said, nodding. "From what I understand, the original protective screen over it was a dome, so it would be round."

"I'm willing to bet," I said, "that the Silicon Suckers know of the exit and have just kept it locked or blocked."

"Worth finding out before going in there," Laverne said, nodding her head. "We'll be watching if you need help."

With that she and Benny both vanished again before I had a chance to ask them why they didn't just go and talk to the Silicon Suckers instead of me. More than likely there was some reason I didn't know about. Just another question I would have to ask later.

Before anyone could say anything, Madge appeared out of the invisible door carrying the thermos of hot chocolate, the most sacred and valuable of drugs to the Silicon Suckers.

I was going to need to negotiate for Laverne's daughter's life with hot chocolate. I just hoped I could offer them enough.

Chapter Five

Five minutes later, after making sure my plan was solid with Stan and Screamer and Patty, I found myself standing alone on the edge of Highway 95 leading north out of Las Vegas.

The Silicon Suckers' main entrance was under a billboard, hidden from view for anyone not welcome in their castles, as they called their caverns and tunnels.

The hot wind was whipping my coat around me and I had to hold my hat on my head with one hand to keep from having to chase it up the highway.

I waited until there were no cars coming in either direction, then slipped off my shoes and left them in the sand next to a sagebrush. I stepped into the wide tunnel and took ten steps into the sand tunnel, as showed respect, then stopped.

Silicon Suckers were big into respect. And rules. They had a million rules.

A few seconds later two Silicon Suckers appeared. They were, as normal, completely naked, but I had no idea what sex they were, or if Silicon Suckers even had a sex. Their bodies were very, very skinny and a pasty gray, but their heads were huge, with wide, unblinking eyes.

Over the centuries, humans who had seen them called them aliens and lately they had become known as the Grays. But as far as I knew, they had lived on Earth longer than humans, and that was going some I was starting to discover.

Both of the Silicon Suckers bowed slightly to me and I returned the bow, then followed them down through what seemed like miles of sandstone tunnels, illuminated but something I had never been able to figure out. The light just seemed to come from everywhere in the tunnel.

When we broke out into the open into the huge cavern that was the main area of this city, I was stunned. Never had I seen so many Silicon Suckers in this area, and they all seemed to be moving at a normal pace, clearly all busy.

From what I understood, hot chocolate not only was a wonderful drug to the Silicon Suckers, but it was a critical element in their health and ability to reproduce. And clearly they had been doing a great deal of reproducing in the year we had been giving them a number of thermoses of hot chocolate every month in payment.

After almost thirty minutes of walking behind my guides, I was shown into a large room I knew to be the Great One's throne room. Only it was as empty as every other room and tunnel I had seen in this place.

I was told to wait and my guides left me standing alone.

Then from one side of the room, a tall and clearly elderly Silicon Sucker appeared and walked slowly toward me. I knew, without a doubt, even though most of the Silicon Suckers looked identical to me, that I was facing their great leader.

I bowed very deeply.

"It is a great honor that you have blessed us once again with your presence, my friend," the Great One said.

"The honor is mine," I said, carefully respecting their tradition. "May I offer the people of this fantastic castle a gift?"

The Great One nodded slightly and I pulled the thermos of hot chocolate from my coat and sat it on the ground in front of me.

Two others came from a side tunnel and carefully picked up the thermos and carried it away.

After they had left, the great one indicated that I should sit and he did the same, facing me.

Then he nodded, a sign I had permission to speak.

"Great One," I said, bowing slightly as was the custom when someone spoke in front of the Great One, "I am honored by your gracious gift of time to listen to me. I have a very serious problem that only you and your wisdom can help me solve."

The Great One just nodded, signaling I could continue.

"Helen, the daughter of Laverne and Benny, two of our greatest leaders, has vanished."

The Great One leaned forward, clearly reacting in some way to my news.

"Helen is such a wonderful child," the Great One said. "Full of spirit, yet very respectful, as are her parents."

I actually was so stunned he knew Helen, I got off my planned script and for a moment sat there not moving.

"Has she gone into the ancient city?" the Great One asked.

"We think she has, oh Great One," I said, bowing again. "And I am afraid we do not know where the exit is."

The Great One said nothing, so I continued on.

"We would be willing to offer four more containers of the sacred liquid per moon cycle for ten sun cycles if you knew where the exit is from the ancient city and would allow my team to enter the city from our entrance, find her, and bring her back to her parents."

"As I would expect of you, your willingness to risk yourself is admirable."

I bowed slightly in acknowledgement of the compliment. However, a sentence like that usually was followed by the word, "But..."

"We will create a special and separate tunnel from the exit of the ancient city to the surface and allow you to use it for ten sun cycles. But for such work and use, we will require six containers per moon cycle."

I sat dead still for a few seconds. I was expected to negotiate. It was a custom.

"Great One," I finally said, "your kind offer is very generous. If I am allowed to make a counter proposal?"

He nodded, so I went on.

"We can only bring five more than we are doing now per moon cycle for the first year. But then, after that, we can add one more per sun cycle for the ten years of the use of the tunnel you are so graciously willing to build."

I was making sure that he understood that we valued our thermoses of hot chocolate as much as he did, even though we did not. And yet I was giving him a chance to continue to let his people grow and multiply.

He nodded slightly. "Your proposal is very fair. We have an agreement. You can enter the ancient city from above at any time. It will take us only a very short amount of time to open the new tunnel from the ancient city exit to the surface."

"The first payment will be at your entrance tomorrow at sunrise and then with the other regular payment every moon cycle."

"It is always an honor," the Great One said to me, bowing slightly.

"The honor is always mine," I said, bowing as deeply as I could while sitting down.

He stood and without another word left the room.

I waited until he was gone before standing. My legs screamed at me for sitting cross-legged on the dirt floor, but I had had no option.

Two guides appeared a moment later and after thirty minutes of sweating in my black leather coat, we had climbed back to the surface.

I grabbed my shoes and an instant later was in the cool air of my new office floating over Las Vegas.

"Well done," Laverne said, looking like she wanted to hug me.

Benny just smiled and nodded.

"We're not done yet," I said as Patty handed me a large glass of water and I took off my black coat. "We still have to find Helen and get her out of that city."

"At least there's a way out now," Laverne said. "Thanks to you and your fantastic thinking. Not sure why someone hadn't thought of that before now."

With that she and Benny vanished and I slumped into the booth to tell the rest of my team what had just happened.

After I was done, Patty gave me a little kiss on the cheek and then squeezed my hand.

"So we're going in," Screamer said, nodding.

I nodded and turned to Stan. "Is there a map of the ancient city?"

"I'll find out," he said, and vanished.

"I thought you had the exit cleared with the Silicon Suckers," Screamer said.

"I do," I said, "But that ancient city is as large as the entire city of Las Vegas. We first have to find Helen. After that, I honestly have no idea where exactly that one door out is."

"Oh," Screamer said, looking shocked again.

I felt the same way.

Chapter Six

Laverne found a very old map of a city that seemed to be not only the size of Las Vegas, but a hundred times larger. In fact, from what I could tell from the old map, at one time the ancient city filled the entire valley.

Stan held that map and the rest of us carried supplies. In packs we had enough food and water to last us a month if we rationed.

We were standing on a side street off of Freemont looking like we were heading into the wilderness for two weeks instead of through a simple door I had never noticed before.

We waited until there was no one on the sidewalk around us, then Stan pulled the door open and held it for us to step through.

I glanced around once more at the city I loved, hoping I

would see it again, then holding Patty's hand, I stepped through and into what looked like a long, simple hallway.

Screamer followed, then Stan who pulled the door closed, plunging us into complete blackness.

Patty was the only one who was thinking and had a flashlight in her hand. She snapped it on and pointed it ahead down the hallway that now looked a great deal like a tunnel.

Now I knew where the ancient city got its nickname of "tunnels."

My stomach was in a tight knot and I could barely breath the stale, dust-smelling air. Only Patty's superpower ability to keep me calm allowed me to move forward. Otherwise I was sure I would have turned and fled for the door and the street beyond.

"Feel that?" Screamer asked.

"Sense of dread spell," Stan said, nodding.

A moment later it was gone as was my need to panic and run. Now all I felt was just plain old fear.

"Thank you," I said.

"Yes," Patty said. "I was barely holding on against it."

"You were doing fine," I said, squeezing her hand as I led us down the hallway and around a corner.

There the beam of her flashlight found another door made of old wood. It had a metal pull handle with strange inscriptions on the metal and the plate under the handle.

"Here we go," Stan said.

I nodded and pulled the door open, sending waves of dust swirling around us in the hallway.

It was now or never.

I stepped through the doorway and into the ancient city.

And stopped cold at what I saw spread out in front of me.

"How can that be?" Patty asked breathlessly beside me.

"Oh, oh," Stan said.

"You have got to be kidding?" Screamer said.

And then, behind us, I heard the door close with a loud thump that sent a chill down my spine.

We were standing on a high balcony with an iron railing protecting us from a very, very long fall. From the looks of it more than thirty or forty stories.

The ancient city was spread out below us. But it wasn't ancient and it certainly wasn't underground and it certainly wasn't empty.

In fact, snow was falling gently on the massive city and I could feel the faint wind and the not-so-faint sounds of a busy city very much alive below us.

We were no longer under Las Vegas.

Or if we were, this was the strangest illusion I had ever seen or felt.

Because we had stepped from a warm afternoon in Las Vegas to a cold, snowy night in a very strange city.

Chapter Seven

As I stared out over the fantastic city, suddenly I wished I had listened a little more carefully when Stan explained to me how my new office was out of time and space a half turn. Because I had a hunch this city was the same.

And if we went down into those streets, I was pretty certain we would meet some real Titans. Or at least the descendents of the real Titans from legend.

I really wished I had studied history and legends more back when I was in school. I just never expected to need it like this.

The city stretching into the light snow looked like a fantastic alien science fiction city you might see in the movies with towering beautiful buildings and walkways crisscrossing from building to building mixed up with an ancient Eastern city with arches and columns and narrow, stone roads.

A huge boulevard wider than The Strip in Vegas wound its way through the city and as far as I could see, lined by sleek glowing buildings that seemed to vanish up into the snow. Futuristic cars that looked like they were polished metal without windows seamlessly flowed up and down the boulevard only on the wrong side of the road as far as I was concerned, like they did in England.

There were a few pedestrians out along the roads, but we were so high in the air I couldn't get any idea of what they looked like.

The snow was thin and the lights from the bustling city made it all seem sort of like I was staring over a fairy tale city inside a snow globe.

For all I knew, I was. I was starting to learn that anything was possible when it came to my world. So maybe we were in a huge snow globe that was the prison to the Titans.

I tried to clear that thought out of my head without much success.

I turned and looked at the door we had come in.

It had vanished. Just a blank, gray cement wall filled the area behind us. No going back that way.

I knew that would be the case, but now being faced with it scared me more than I wanted to admit.

And I had a hunch that finding the exit from this huge city wasn't going to be easy.

We had all stood there on that high balcony in silence for a good minute before I squeezed Patty's hand and turned to Stan. "Got any idea how we might find Helen in this place?"

"I know exactly where she's at," he said, shaking his head and coming back to our situation.

"That's good," Screamer asked. "But anyone besides Poker Boy here think to bring a coat?"

For the first time I noticed just how cold it was. Even my black leather coat didn't cut the chill.

An instant later all of us were wearing heavy parkas of varying colors. Patty's was a stylish pink, mine was plain and black like my leather jacket under it, so it matched my fedora-like black hat. Screamer's coat was green with deep pockets that he instantly stuck his hands into. Stan had put himself in a blue parka with a hood and gloves.

I was glad he hadn't given me and Patty gloves. I got a lot of strength from her touch.

"That help?" Stan asked, smiling.

"Thanks," Patty said.

"So how do you know where Helen is at here?" I asked Stan.

"We have a connection when we are close in distance," Stan said. "I've kind of ignored it for years, but it's still there."

"A connection?" Patty asked.

Stan nodded, turning to stare out over the beautiful and very alien city around us. "We were married once."

I just stared at my boss like he had become an alien.

Stan had been married to Lady Luck's daughter. That must have been some divorce.

"Can you jump us to her?" Patty asked, since I hadn't said anything.

He nodded and a moment later we were standing in the snow in what looked like a garden surrounded by stone walls. A brown stone patio filled the center of the garden and in the background was a singly-story home with warm orange lights coming from the windows.

The most stunning, redheaded woman I had ever seen was smiling at us.

She wore a white dress that looked more like a thin night-gown. It sort of drifted around her frame and blew in the wind. She had to be cold since I was pretty certain I was seeing through most of that dress or nightgown or whatever it was.

She moved barefooted in the snow across the stone of the patio toward us, her bright red hair blowing in the wind.

All of us stood frozen as she approached and kissed Stan in such a way that most of the snow in the garden area must have melted.

Then she broke the kiss and said, "Wonderful to see you again, my husband."

"Ex-husband," Stan said.

She ignored him and extended her hand to me. "I'm Helen. You must be Poker Boy."

I'm not sure if it was the thin blowing white dress around the naked body in the snow, or her radiant smile, but something caused me to pause before extending my hand as well. "Nice to meet you."

Then Helen turned to Patty. "The famous Patty Ledger-wood I presume."

"An honor," Patty said, shaking Helen's hand.

Then Helen turned to Screamer and nodded and said nothing.

"Nice seeing you again as well, Sheila," Screamer said, smiling.

I managed to take my eyes off of Helen long enough to look at Screamer with a puzzled look. Clearly he had met her before, only she had called herself Sheila to him.

Wow, did I have a lot of questions when we got out of here.

The woman in the thin, white blowing dress seemed like no Sheila I had ever met.

Screamer just kept his eyes on Helen, and she shrugged and smiled at him.

The next moment we all were inside in a warm living room with a crackling fire in a huge stone fireplace. Helen now had on regular jeans and a flannel shirt and her hair was pulled back. It didn't decrease her beauty in any respect. But it sure made her seem far more human.

Outside in the snow, she had been a goddess. Now she seemed almost normal, if that was possible.

I pretty much doubted it.

The room around us reminded me of a mountain lodge, with warm-brown logs as walls and high ceilings with log rafters. Tan overstuffed couches and chairs surrounded the fireplace and a couple of scarred coffee tables filled the center area.

The air had a faint smoke smell from the burning logs and every-so-often the fire would pop or crackle.

Thick, dark-brown carpet covered all of the floor except a stone area in front of the fireplace. The carpet added to the feeling of warmth in the room.

I could spend a lot of time in a place like this, especially if it was snowing outside.

"Nice entrance," Stan said to her as he pulled off his parka and dropped down onto a couch.

"You know I always play the part, dear husband," Helen said, laughing. "Thought I was going to freeze off a part or two for a moment there."

"Ex-husband," Stan said more to himself.

"It was a show all right," Screamer said, taking off his parka as well.

"I thought it impressive," Patty said as we both took off our coats and sat on a couch facing Stan.

"Thank you," Helen said, nodding to Patty.

Screamer moved to a chair near the fireplace and Helen sat alone in a large, overstuffed chair facing all of us.

"So did you find what you came for?" Stan asked Helen, his voice clearly telling me he wasn't into any idle chatting, even though I had about a thousand questions I would have loved to have answered at that moment.

Helen smiled and her eyes lit up like a child's eyes with a new toy. "And what do you think I came for?"

"One of the keys of Janus," Stan said.

She laughed, a perfect laugh that might draw someone from across a room. "I did. I had researched it well and knew exactly where it was hidden. I found it within twenty minutes of arriving here."

"And how did you plan on getting back with it?" Screamer asked, also clearly not interested in just having a social visit.

She turned to me, then glanced at Stan. "I knew Mother and Dad would send a rescue party. And I knew it would be you and Poker Boy and his team. And I knew Poker Boy knew the Silicon Suckers and would bargain with them to open the exit, since I am pretty sure the exit has to go into their territory."

She turned to me. "You did that, didn't you?"

"I did," I said, stunned that she had played us like I played a sucker at a poker table.

"Great," she said, clapping her hands together. "Then let's get out of here before the Titans discover some of the Gods are among them. I have a hunch they won't like that much."

"Do you know where the exit is at?" I asked.

Helen looked at me like I now had two heads. "No. Don't you?"

I shook my head. "The Silicon Suckers just promised me it would be open with a tunnel to the surface. They never showed me where it was."

She turned to Stan.

"Sorry," he said.

She looked at Screamer.

"We didn't even know this city was here," he said. "We thought we were going into ancient ruins to look for you."

"Oh, no," Helen said, slumping in her chair and covering her face with her hands.

I glanced at Patty, then back at Helen, the Queen of Hearts.

Looks like there was one little detail the Queen of Hearts hadn't figured out in her little scheme.

A very important one.

Chapter Eight

Actually, what she hadn't been thinking about, I had, from the very first moment I learned that Laverne wanted us to go down into the "tunnels" as this city was called by those who had never been here.

I wondered what people who lived in this beautiful place actually called it. And exactly where it was in reality. It certainly wasn't under Las Vegas.

"Okay, a couple of questions," I said to the group sitting silently around the fire. "Where exactly is this city in time and space? And what the heck is it called?"

Stan shrugged and looked at Helen.

"The city's name is Elysium," she said without looking up. "It exists in a time in the distant future from what I understand."

Patty coughed, glanced at me, then asked, "Elysium, like in Elysium Fields, like in a form of heaven?"

Helen shrugged. "All myth and rumors of this place. But it is actually a pretty nice city from what I have seen of it."

"Great, just great," Screamer said. "We haven't died and we're stuck in heaven."

I didn't know what to think about her answer. Something was nagging at me, but darned if I could figure it out. Something about this city being in the far future, yet we had come into it in our time, and it seemed to have a protected area in our time as well, under Las Vegas.

Maybe it really was a city inside a giant snow globe buried under Las Vegas.

Again I tried to clear my mind of that stupid thought.

I needed to ask another hundred or more questions, but like everything with this rescue mission so far, most of the questions were going to have to wait until after we got out of here.

If we got out of here.

So I picked the one question that bothered me the most.

"So when we came through the door, we stepped into the future?"

"I believe we did," Helen said, then sighed and slumped in the chair like a kid not getting her way.

The future. That was the key. I had an idea. It wasn't much of one, but it was all I had at the moment.

I stood and started to put my parka back on over my black

leather coat. "Stan, could you jump us back to the balcony we came in on?"

He looked at me with that studying look that only the God of Poker could give a person, then nodded and stood and put on his coat as well.

Screamer shrugged and did the same and so did Patty.

"I'll be right here when you get back," Helen said. "I'm still chilled from my last little adventure out there."

Stan just shook his head and a moment later we were standing on the balcony looking through the snow and out over the beautiful city below.

The cold air hit my face with a bite, but actually it felt good and cleared my thoughts even more. The wind swirled the light snow through the buildings and now there seemed to be very few people on the streets below. Whatever the local time was, it must be getting late.

Back in Vegas it wasn't even dinnertime yet.

Patty took my hand and I could feel her calming influence push through me.

I looked at the blank wall behind me where the door from Las Vegas into this city had been.

"So what are you thinking, Poker Boy?" Screamer asked.

I pointed at where the door had been. "We came in level to Freemont Street in downtown Vegas. Right?"

Everyone nodded, so I turned and pointed down. "We have to be a good thirty stories above the street level here. And we know the exit is underground and against the Silicon Sucker's territory."

"So more than likely it's down on the main city level somewhere," Screamer said. "That's a lot of area to look for a door that is more than likely very hidden."

"I agree," I said.

I turned to my boss. "Stan, is it possible in our vision or in our minds, whatever, to overlay a view of Las Vegas from our time over this city? Same scale and everything?"

He looked at me and actually frowned. "We would need to be connected."

"Screamer?"

He nodded and I indicated everyone should step to the metal railing of the balcony and face out over the city. Screamer stood between me and Stan and Patty had my hand on the other side.

Screamer's main power was the ability to hook up thoughts, to see what others were seeing with a touch.

He touched my hand and suddenly he and I and Patty were all together again in my head. We had done this so many times over the last few years, I sometimes wondered if them being in my mind wasn't more comfortable than when they weren't there.

I like it too, Patty thought at me.

Me, not so much, Screamer thought back.

Then Screamer touched Stan and brought the God of Poker into the mix. And instantly a map of Las Vegas formed in my vision. Actually, more than a map, an image of the city as if we were in the air over the downtown area where we had gone through the door.

Rotate it so that the Strip is running along that big boule-vard below, I thought to Stan.

He did, and suddenly the two main roads overlaid almost perfectly, only the one in this city kept going out into the distance, right through where the airport had been in our time.

This is a future Las Vegas, Screamer thought, clearly stunned.

"Stan, take us north, keeping the cities lined up, along our Highway 95 where the Silicon Suckers home castle is."

Suddenly we were no longer on the balcony, but instead flying through the snow with an image of Vegas below us overlapping the streets and boulevards of Elysian.

It was even colder up in the air like this. My face and hands were going to take some warming time when this was over. I just hoped my nose didn't freeze off.

I'd still love you anyway, Patty thought.

Knock it off you two, Screamer thought.

Stan took us north slowly until finally I indicated he should stop.

We were right over the edge of the Silicon Sucker's bound-ary. And clearly they still lived there, since there was nothing but huge mounds of sand and empty spaces over their Terri-tory. The mounds of sand towered into the air over the edge of the new city.

The Silicon Suckers still exist, Patty thought, feeling as stunned as I felt.

I pointed to a wooden shack that had been built against

the huge mound of sand. It looked very, very old and weathered. And sand covered the back half of the building. And on the front, facing the city, was a closed wooden door.

Is that the door home? Screamer asked in a thought that felt excited.

I could sense Patty was excited as well.

It might be, I thought back. *It would have been a long ways underground in our time. Stan, take us along the edge of the Silicon Sucker's territory to the west and then back to the east.*

We spent the next five cold minutes drifting through the air, the map of our time imposed over the city below. Then we ended up back over the old shack half buried in the sand.

We had found nothing else touching the Silicon Sucker's territory.

Looks like we might have found our door out, I thought to the others.

Part of me wanted to shout for joy.

And part of me was scared to death that we were wrong.

CHAPTER NINE

An instant later we were back in the warm room with Helen and the wonderful crackling fire.

Screamer dropped his grip on my arm and I was again alone inside my head.

"Any luck?" Helen asked.

"Maybe," Stan said to her. "Get on a coat and gather your things."

She jumped to her feet like an excited child and vanished.

Patty and I moved over in front of the crackling fire, holding our hands closer to the flames in a sad attempt to warm them.

In less than fifteen seconds Helen was back, bundled in a heavy coat with a bag over her shoulder. With a wave of her hand, the fire went out, the lights in the place dimmed, and white sheets covered the furniture.

"Planning on returning?" Screamer asked.

"You never know," Helen said.

An instant later Stan had us standing in the desert in front of the old shack. The wind was blowing harder here and the snow felt like small grains of sand against my cheeks.

Up close the door looked very similar to the one we had come through on the way in. Same rough metal handle with strange inscriptions, same old wood. That made me feel a little more hopeful.

I turned to face everyone and held up my hand for attention. Then shouting over the wind I said, "If this is our door out and we end up in the Silicon Sucker's tunnels on the other side, it is critical we say nothing and calmly walk to the surface."

I looked directly at Helen and she looked back, very puzzled.

She then started to say something and Stan held up his hand. "If you can't agree to Poker Boy's instructions, you stay here."

"And how can you make me do that?" Helen demanded, her eyes blazing as she turned to face her ex-husband.

She was so angry, I had no doubt that the snow wasn't getting near her. I know I wanted to step back, but I didn't.

Stan just kept his poker face and said calmly, "We will go through first and make sure the Silicon Suckers never open the exit again."

"You would do that to me?"

"I would," Stan said. "And I am sure your parents, once

they know you are alive and living just fine, would agree with me."

She started to say something and then closed her mouth. She turned her back on Stan, staring at the wooden door in front of her. Her face was bright red, almost matching her hair blowing in the wind.

"It is critical we say nothing and walk to the surface," I said again, looking directly at her and keeping my voice as even as I can. "Please? The Silicon Suckers have opened this tunnel for us. The least we can do is honor their customs in their land."

Finally, she took a deep breath and nodded.

I glanced past her at Stan and he nodded. I had a hunch he was going to make sure she followed the instructions. I didn't want to think of dealing with the Silicon Suckers again if he couldn't keep her under control.

I took a couple steps through the sand and pulled on the door. It didn't move.

Stan stepped up and made a motion and then pulled the door open, scraping back sand as he did.

A dark concrete tunnel lead into the mound of sand inside the small shack and again Patty snapped on her flashlight and I lead the way, holding her hand.

Screamer followed us, then Helen, and Stan came in last, pulling the outside door closed behind us.

We walked silently for about thirty paces and then around a corner to face another door.

I indicated everyone keep quite with a finger against my lips, then I pushed the door open.

Beyond the door was a sand tunnel that I knew was dug by the Silicon Suckers. It had the same light that seemed to come from everywhere and the same scraping marks on the walls.

But the question was had we gone back in time or were we just walking inside a Silicon Suckers' tunnel in the future without invite?

Patty instantly snapped off her flashlight and put it away.

I lead the way up the steep slope of the tunnel, only glancing back to make sure Helen was still with us and that Stan had closed the door.

There were no side tunnels at all.

The climb had to be the longest in my life. But actually it took us less than ten minutes until the tunnel leveled and I walked out into the evening light and warmth of the desert outside of Las Vegas.

A bright red Ford pickup truck sped past on Highway 95.

As Patty stepped into the evening sun, Laverne and Benny appeared, both looking happy and angry at the same time. I didn't want to think about what this family meeting was going to be like.

As Helen stepped into the light, a bright smile crossed her face as she saw her parents. Then she turned to Stan.

"You can take off the shield now holding me here," she said.

"Not me," Stan said, smiling.

Helen turned to stare at her parents. "Mom?"

"We'll talk," she said.

And with that Helen vanished, and not to a place she wanted to go I would wager.

"Thank you again," Lady Luck said and behind her Benny nodded.

It never got old having Lady Luck thank you.

Lady Luck went on. "After we get family business taken care of, I would love to hear about your adventure on the other side. I'll come join you all for lunch one of these days."

Then she and Benny vanished as the four of us stood there with our mouths open.

An instant later Stan had us back in my office and we were all missing our parkas.

And I had about six thousand questions built up to ask.

Screamer shook his head and looked out at Las Vegas below my office. "Well, that was an interesting afternoon trip. I think there's a steak with my name on it at the MGM Grand."

"Mind if I join you?" Stan asked. "I would love to know how you knew Helen or Sheila, as you called her."

"You drive," Screamer said, smiling, and an instant later they were both gone.

Without answering a single question I had.

"So that leaves just the two of us," Patty said, looking at me with those big brown eyes of hers. "Any ideas?"

"Maybe trying to find out what just happened? And what

those keys were all about. And why exactly that city is there. And who did it."

"More than enough time for that," Patty said, smiling. "I'm going to call in and cancel work tonight. I think they can get by without me, don't you?"

I took a deep breath and looked out over the city I loved. I was finally starting to catch her drift. It was time to celebrate being back and being alive.

"I do," I said, nodding seriously.

"Then after I call work I want to take a long hot shower," she said, smiling at me and giving me a quick kiss. "I'm still chilled. Then maybe some dinner."

"Mind if I join you?" I asked, holding her close. "I'm sure they can get along without me at the poker tournament tonight as well."

"For dinner?" she asked.

"I was thinking of the shower to be honest," I said.

"You drive," she said, smiling.

"With pleasure," I said.

And it turned out that with pleasure was a very good description of the rest of the evening.

The Fun Starts Here

Just Turn The Page...

SNEAK PEEK

Being Dead (The First Year)

CHAPTER ONE

Dying on a first date sucks.

Dying on a blind date sucks even worse.

Especially when your date dies with you. And then goes off through some tunnel of light into the next life or something, leaving you sitting alone, dead, in a dark alley, waiting for your own tunnel of light.

Hands down, the worst ending to any date in recorded history.

The alley we had been forced to go into was blacker than the inside of a latrine, and seeing how it smelled, I would have not been surprised to be in a latrine, but I knew I wasn't since it seemed that being dead meant I could see just fine in the dark.

And smell just fine as well. Holy crap. The nearby Chinese restaurant garbage smelled like my fridge after six days of feeling sorry for myself and laying on the couch and eating take-out without taking out the uneaten food in the original cartons. And no telling how many homeless and drunks had actually used this alley for a bathroom.

I was sitting on a big green dumpster owned by a nearby office, so thankfully it didn't have the odor of the other dumpsters coming up between my legs.

The scum with the greasy black hair and dirty ski parka that had killed us was going through my date's pockets as I sat and watched.

The guy looked skinny and no doubt drug-addicted. His motions were jerky, his eyes darting around him like a rat trying to find a way out of a maze.

My blind date, dear old Handsome Bob, as I had started to think of him for the full thirty minutes I had known him, had caused this mess by thinking he could be a macho asshole or something.

The scum with the greasy black hair had approached us on the sidewalk and Bob had shaken his head and said, "Not now."

We were headed down the street to a nice Italian restaurant that served the best red wine and bread plate this side of New York. And that was going some for the Old Towne section of Boise, Idaho.

Bob was dressed in a clearly expensive silk suit and no tie, while I didn't look so cheap myself. For the date I had put on dark slacks, a white silk blouse with pearls around my neck, and a thin see-through sweater. No bra because I wanted my date to get an occasional peek at what might be offered after dinner if things went right.

Sitting dead in an alley sure wasn't my idea of things going right.

The greasy jerk had pulled out a gun, his hands shaking. Dear old dead Handsome Bob had said, "You don't want to do that."

Bless him.

Clearly the druggie did want to do exactly what he was doing, but I didn't say that. I was busy ramping up one of my super powers.

You see, before I was so suddenly cut down, I had worked as a superhero in the housing and hotel industry. Over the last century I had worked both front desks of hotels and sold real estate. At the moment I was on the real estate side, trying to help out in the booming Boise real estate market.

Amazing the kind of crap that goes on in real estate when big money is involved.

I hit greasy-hair with a full dose of my calming power. The guy was so high on drugs my power actually didn't do anything but make him stop shaking so hard.

He pointed to the dark alley with the gun. "Get in there and then dig out your money."

"And if we say no?" Handsome Bob asked the guy.

Since Bob was almost a foot taller than the greasy-haired druggie, I suppose Bob thought he could bully the situation a little.

Bless dear old now-dead stupid Bob.

I hit the guy with another dose of calming power. I had enough power on a normal day to stop a shouting, irate, pissed-off hotel customer at a front desk and make them smile.

The guy with the gun got calmer, but his pea brain was still set on robbing us. At least I got him to not shoot us right there on the sidewalk because of Handsome Bob's stupidity.

"Let's just give him our stuff and he will let us go," I said to Bob.

"Smart woman," the guy said, smiling and showing a mouthful of rotted teeth.

Actually, I had planned that when we got into the alley I would simply jump us away from this nut and then figure out something to tell dear old Bob.

Bob didn't know I was a one-hundred-year-old superhero and could just teleport anywhere I wanted. Not something you tell someone before a first blind date. Men tended to have sexual problems when they realized the woman they were with was over a hundred.

Bob nodded to me and we walked the twenty steps into the alley, Bob pushing me slightly ahead of him.

Then, as we stopped and turned at just about the point where the rotted Chinese food odor got the worst, Bob went to lunge at the guy.

Handsome Bob went to really, really stupid Bob very quickly.

I was so surprised Bob would do something that idiotic, I didn't react fast enough to jump us out of there.

The guy fired, hitting Bob in the arm.

The bullet went through Bob's flesh and hit me square between the eyes.

Now that was a shocker, let me tell you.

One moment I am standing alive in the alley and the next I am a ghost sitting on a smelly dumpster watching dear old Handsome Bob hold his arm and swear.

The greasy-haired guy was now twitching again. He stared at my body lying there in the alley, clearly getting my wonderful blouse and sweater all stained up with my own blood.

Then he looked at Bob, who was also staring at me, holding his wounded arm and looking sick to his stomach.

Then the guy did what any self-respecting murderer would do. He shot Bob.

Bob slumped to the ground and the guy fired one more shot into Bob's head.

A moment later I watched Bob's ghost stand up, look around, then look up and float off into a white light.

"Nice meeting you jerk-face," I shouted after Bob.

I was pretty sure he didn't hear me.

As I said, the worst ending to a blind date ever.

Chapter Two

The druggie who had killed me and my blind date started through Bob's pockets. The druggie pulled out a money clip and then took Bob's watch. Then he rolled Bob over slightly and took out his wallet.

He pulled out a single-package condom and tossed it aside.

I just shook my head. "Damn, Bob, only one? Where was the confidence? If you had come back to my place, you would have needed at least three just to make it to breakfast."

The greasy murderer clearly didn't hear me. And I had a hunch dead Bob didn't either.

I glanced around. I was still the only ghost in the alley.

Where was my greeting party?

I figured I had become a Ghost Agent, which was why I hadn't gotten the beam-of-light ride. I had never met a Ghost

Agent, but I had heard from my best friend Patty that she and her boyfriend, Poker Boy, had worked with some Ghost Agents just lately to save the world. Seems Patty and her boyfriend were always saving the world, which I must admit I appreciated.

The guy stood and stepped toward my body.

"Hey, not so fast there, jerk-face," I said, jumping down from the dumpster and brushing off my pants.

The greasy-haired slime-ball picked up my clutch purse and went through it. That I didn't much care about. I had a few hundred in there and that was that.

But then he looked around at the mouth of the alley and then looked back at me with that look I had seen scum like him get. Ghost or no ghost, he wasn't touching me, even if I did have a hole in the middle of my forehead.

This night had gone bad enough as it was.

The guy kneeled down beside my body and I took two quick steps at the guy and went to kick him clear across the alley.

Foot went right through him. Charlie Brown would have been proud of my form, though. I didn't end up on my back.

However, when my foot went through the guy, I got to read all of his thoughts.

All of what he was about to do to me.

So I closed my eyes and went inside the scum. Now I knew for a fact I was in a cesspool, swimming in the shit that this guy called thoughts. If I got out of here I would need about ten showers.

If ghosts took showers.

As he reached for my right breast, I shouted at the top of my lungs, "No!"

And trust me, I can be loud.

Just ask anyone who sat beside me at a Broncos' football game.

And I was inside the guy when I shouted.

Slime-bucket grabbed his head and rolled over backward, the intense pain striking everywhere.

As he rolled away, I managed to stand my ground and get out of his body. I shook myself, wishing I could forget the memories of what I had just seen in his mind.

It would take twenty showers before I would feel clean again.

The guy was holding his head and screaming and rolling on the ground. Blood was coming out of his ears.

Both ears.

"Wow, what did you do to him?" a voice behind me asked.

I turned around to see a handsome couple standing to one side looking shocked. Both were about my height of five-ten, both wore jeans, expensive shirts, and tennis shoes.

"The pervert was about to get his jollies on my dead body, so I climbed inside his head and shouted as loud as I could."

Both of them laughed.

Then the woman stepped forward. "I'm Jewel and this is Tommy. We came to help get you used to being a ghost, but guess you are doing just fine."

I shook both their hands, happy as hell I had company.

"I'm Marble Grant. And got a hunch I'm going to need a lot of help."

"Someone close to you?" Tommy asked, pointing at Handsome Bob.

"Knew him for thirty minutes," I said. "Blind date. But I had planned on getting much closer to him after dinner, if you get my drift."

Jewel laughed and Tommy actually blushed a little, which I loved. I had a feeling I was going to like these two.

"I suppose you two are Ghost Agents. Right?"

Both of them looked shocked.

"I was a superhero in the hospitality and real estate side of the world," I said. "Any chance you two know Patty Ledgerwood and Poker Boy?"

"We do," Jewel said.

"You know," I said, "I'm damn hungry and I assume there is a way ghosts eat, so any chance we could get out of this smell and grab a bite and you guys call Patty and have her meet us. I would kind of like to tell her about my sudden death myself, since she has been my best friend for a hundred years now, give or take."

Both of them just nodded.

"Anything we need to do with that guy?" I asked, looking down at the scum who had killed me and Handsome Bob before I had the chance to find out if the handsome part went all the way to Bob's southern regions.

Greasy hair was still rolling on the dirty concrete, holding his ears and screaming. He was losing a lot of blood through his fingers. I clearly had done some damage.

"I think he's finished," Tommy said, laughing.

"Yeah," Jewel said. "Got to remember that trick."

With that we jumped to a place I knew well and loved, the Golden Nugget Buffet in downtown Las Vegas.

Now I knew I was really going to like these two.

Chapter Three

The Golden Nugget Buffet had been decorated in all warm brown cloth and polished brass. Plants ringed the outside of the side part of the dining room nearest the escalator and the tables were solid, as were the chairs.

My hand went right through a chair as I tried to pull it out and Jewel did it for me.

"You'll learn how to actually move some physical matter, but you don't want to do that too often because people start to get spooked."

"I'll bet," I said.

Tommy jumped away to find Patty, and Jewel led me up to the wonderful smelling food. The images from the murderer's head were slowly fading, something I was very grateful for.

"Be careful to not run into anyone," Jewel said, indicating the six people around the large buffet area. "You end up reading their thoughts."

"Yeah, learned that with the guy who shot me," I said.

Jewel showed me how to pick up a plate, which was actually just the ghost component of the plate, and how to take food from the buffet.

In five minutes of filling a ghost plate with ghost food, I managed to not run into anyone alive, which sort of felt like a victory. I called it the dance of the living. A living person came toward me, I stepped sideways and went around them.

Jewel did the same, seemingly without noticing.

Back at the table, I bit into a piece of prime rib and damn near had an orgasm right there at the table.

Jewel just smiled as I moaned and kept on eating the fantastic tasting food.

"I remember the food being good here," I said after a few bites, "but never this good."

"Everything is better when you are a ghost," Jewel said. "Food tastes better, emotions are more powerful, and the travel and living is easier."

"Sex?" I asked.

"As the joke goes," Jewel said, smiling, "it's to die for."

"Oh, no," I said. "I had enough trouble controlling myself when I was alive."

Jewel just laughed and at that moment Tommy appeared.

"Patty is in Poker Boy's office," Tommy said. "Let's just

grab some food and jump there. She's expecting us but doesn't know why yet."

It dawned on me why Patty couldn't jump here. She was still alive. Anyone in the restaurant would see her arrive and then talk to no one. Not a good idea.

Tommy headed for the buffet. I really needed to pee, but instead I kept eating as we waited for him. Damn, the food was so good. I was going to be lucky to not gain a ton of weight now that I had died. I needed to remember to ask Jewel and Tommy how they stayed so thin.

After Tommy came back with a full plate of food, he jumped the three of us and our food and drink to what I assumed was Poker Boy's office, although I had never been there.

In fact, the place was like a legend.

But I had heard it was something special and I had heard right. The office wasn't really an office. It was more like a tile platform floating in the air a thousand feet over the Strip.

All four walls were freaking clear glass with a wood railing about waist high all the way around.

Without that railing, I would have been so afraid of falling off that slick checkered tile floor, I would have been clinging to the furniture and screaming like a ten-year-old girl not wanting to go see her uncle.

And I was dead, so pretty certain the fall wouldn't kill me again.

Still, scary damn place and now I really had to pee.

I made my heart stop racing and looked around.

In the very center of the room was this huge 1950s style diner booth, with a scarred tabletop and red vinyl booth seats on three sides. The thing was big enough to hold ten people if the people really liked each other.

There were half-a-dozen chairs around the room that could be pulled up to the open end of the booth I suppose, but three of them just sat facing out over the incredible view of the city.

And wow, what a view. I had always loved the lights of Las Vegas. Just never seen them from the air like this before.

"Marble," Patty said as we appeared. "Tommy said you needed to talk with me. Everything all right? You could have just called you know?"

"Not sure I knew how exactly," I said, smiling at my best friend.

Jewel laughed as she set her food and mine on the booth table.

Patty was wearing her MGM Grand Front Desk uniform of dark slacks, tan blouse and a lighter tan vest. She had her long hair pulled back and was as stunning as ever.

Patty frowned, something I had rarely seen her do in a century.

I glanced at my food on the booth table, then turned back to my friend. "Got myself killed while on a blind date about thirty minutes ago."

Patty's eyes went totally round. "Are you all right?"

"Pretty sure I'm dead," I said, laughing. I pointed to my forehead. "Bullet right there did the trick."

Patty looked like she was about to cry.

"Can I hug her?" I asked, glancing back at Jewel.

"She's a superhero," Jewel said, "and she can see you, so sure, don't know why not?"

I stepped toward Patty and she hugged me so hard, I wasn't sure I would be able to breathe.

And I hugged her back.

I guess, for the first time, it was sinking in that I had really died.

I was still here but I was dead.

That just sucked.

Except for the part about the food tasting so much better.

FINISH READING
BEING DEAD (THE FIRST YEAR): A MARBLE GRANT NOVEL

Get More Marble Grant

DeanWesleySmithStore.com

Hear From Dean

Want More From Dean?

For Dean Wesley Smith's newsletter
go to deanwesleysmith.com.

Get the latest news and releases from all of WMG's authors
and lines, including Kristine Grayson, Kris Nelscott,
Pulphouse Magazine, and so much more...

To sign up, **go to wmgbooks.com.**

Considered one of the most prolific writers working in modern fiction, *New York Times* and *USA Today* bestselling writer, Dean Wesley Smith published over two hundred novels and over seven hundred books in forty years, and hundreds and hundreds of short stories. He has over thirty million copies of his books in print.

At the moment he produces novels in four major series, including the time travel **Thunder Mountain** novels set in the old west, the galaxy-spanning **Seeders Universe** series, the cold case mystery series, **Cold Poker Gang** series, and the superhero series staring **Poker Boy.**

During his career, Dean also wrote a couple dozen *Star Trek* novels, the only two original *Men in Black* novels, Spider-Man and X-Men novels, plus novels set in gaming and television worlds. Writing with his wife Kristine Kathryn Rusch under the name Kathryn Wesley, they wrote the novel for the NBC miniseries **The Tenth Kingdom** and other books for *Hallmark Hall of Fame* movies.

He wrote novels under dozens of pen names in the worlds

of comic books and movies, including novelizations of almost a dozen films, from *X-Men* to *The Final Fantasy* to *Steel* to *Rundown.*

Dean also worked as a fiction editor off and on, starting at Pulphouse Publishing, then at *VB Tech Journal*, then Pocket Books, and now at WMG Publishing where he and Kristine Kathryn Rusch serve as executive editors for the acclaimed *Fiction River* anthology series. He took over the editorship of the acclaimed *Pulphouse Magazine* in 2018.

For more information about Dean's books and ongoing projects, please visit his website at www.deanwesleysmith.com

facebook.com/deanwsmith3

patreon.com/deanwesleysmith

bookbub.com/authors/dean-wesley-smith